GW00357399

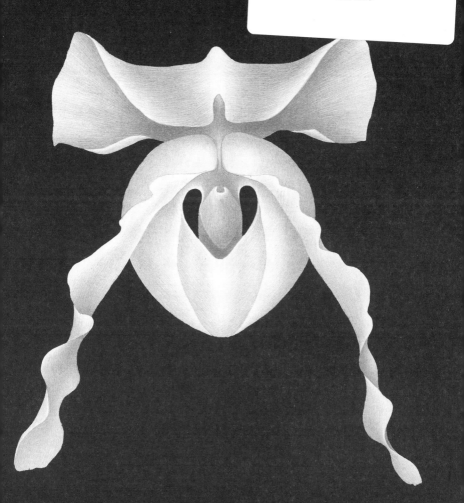

ABERRANT

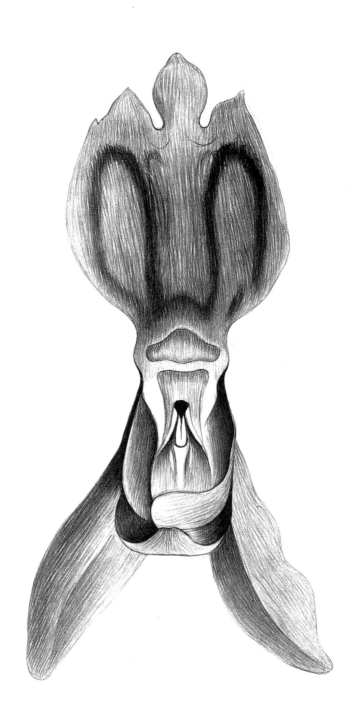

MAREK ŠINDELKA

ABERRANT

Translated from the Czech by Nathan Fields

Artwork by Petr Nikl

TWISTED SPOON PRESS

PRAGUE

2017

ISBN 978-80-86264-50-9

This translation was made possible by a grant
from the Ministry of Culture of the Czech Republic.

MINISTERSTVO
KULTURY

CONTENTS

KRYŠTOF

Kryštof's life ended in the same place it had once begun. This escaped his notice at the time of his death as he had plenty else to worry about. Several things occupied his mind at once. He was trying to use his last moments of lucidity to understand what was actually happening to him. The world around him had melted into a strange uniform mass that seared his insides with every breath he took. As if he were breathing in chlorinated water. He was drowning in it, ingesting it, trying with each gulp to free up space for a bubble of fresh air that never came. Something exploded in his veins. As if he'd taken too much of a drug. *Golden overdose* flashed through his mind. He stopped fighting it. He gave in because he had no other choice. He took deep breaths of the outside world, now only a vague concept to him. All his senses had been rendered practically useless. A dizzying feeling of strange and unknown pleasure washed over him. He leaned his head back and opened his mouth, creating a pathway for the agony flowing through him from the tips of his toes to the top of his head. He exhaled into the universe — and perhaps somewhere even more distant . . .

After an eternity, he felt rain falling into his gaping mouth. He no longer had the strength to close it. He fell asleep. Rain closed his eyes and placed upon them two fluid coins as fare for his trip to the opposite shore.

Kryštof's life began (as he perceived it) with his earliest memory.

It went something like this: They were taking the train somewhere. He and his mom. Evening. End of summer. Speed. Countryside near the Polish border. The compartment smelled of iron, imitation leather, linoleum flooring. He was standing on the armrest of the seat, choking down the draft of wind rushing alongside the train. Chills ran down his back as he felt the wind weave itself into his hair. The sun went down behind the forests of spruce on the hills, and a chill spread over the countryside. The fragrance of the river. A long expanse of fields. The train slowed, gradually decelerated, eventually settling into a footpace. Then it happened.

They entered a forest. A strange forest. It took his breath away. Even his mother turned to get a better look at the odd trees. Kryštof felt her unconsciously tighten her grip on his arm. Windows being pulled down clattered through the train as the curious passengers sought a view better than the one through greasy, scratched glass. Massive stalks of unknown plants with white and bizarrely branching umbels flashed past them. Veined branches of a deep green, sometimes brindled violet, grew from thick stems regularly spaced with huge flowers at their pinnacles. A pungent odor spread through the compartment. Stifling like in a pigsty. Strangely salty.

"That's hogweed," Mother told him.

He repeated the name to himself several times in his mind.

"Kryštof, never . . . listen . . . NEVER play with these plants, do you understand?"

He nodded.

"They are very poisonous," she explained. "The juice inside them will burn your skin. Once Grandpa was cutting them down in the field and the juice got onto his arm . . . He had a blister the size of a tomato for the next six months!"

Kryštof winced. He imagined a tomato growing on his grand-father's arm.

Though he couldn't know it then, he was looking at the precise spot where he would die twenty-four years later.

Hogweed. Never again would that word leave Kryštof's head. He was afraid of the plant for the rest of his childhood. He feared it as if it were a dangerous animal. He feared it would grow in their house in Prague. Maybe in the cellar, or in the hallway, and they wouldn't be able to escape. It gave him nightmares. His mother comforted him by saying that nothing of the sort could possibly happen, that hogweed couldn't grow in the city, but this hardly soothed him. For Kryštof they were not plants, but phantoms in the guise of plants. Countless nights he spent frozen in horror beneath the blanket, immobilized by fear, nearly suffocating from breathing the same stale air. He was too afraid to leave himself even the smallest opening. He knew a poisonous root or a sharp ravenous leaf could creep in and grab him.

Hogweed. Anything he heard or learned about the plant later in life lodged itself deep in his memory, gnawing down through the sediment of all his other experiences until it reached his earliest memory and settled there. The plant demarcated his life. He never understood why this was the one detail he remembered from the trip. In fact, he and his mother were on their way to visit his father then. Why did Kryštof not remember him? Why did he not remember anything else from that time? Kryštof didn't know. August 25, 2002, was his chance to understand this, but again, he was occupied with other matters.

•

Antonín Brom was called off the case. Health problems prevented him from continuing the investigation. His condition quickly deteriorated. He died less than two weeks later from a yet unidentified virulent disease. Hospitalized shortly after being relieved of duty, Brom was not able to complete the report on the current status of his investigation. The case documentation was incomplete. It might even be assumed that Brom intentionally withheld part of it. Though purely speculation, he might have become too personally involved in the case and was searching for something that he had intentionally left out of the dossier.

A rather limited amount of material was left to work with. In order to reconstruct as accurately as possible the circumstances surrounding Warjak's case, all available resources have been utilized, including Brom's personal diary, where he kept relatively detailed notes on how the investigation was proceeding (unfortunately incomplete and unsystematic).

•

Copies of two letters were found folded in Antonín Brom's diary, (the originals are saved as attachment No. 4 in the case file of Kryštof Warjak).

The first letter, sent on August 26, 2002, is addressed to Dr. Josef Podlipský, a specialist in Asian flora, with a focus on endangered species of the Japanese islands, and a former employee of the Botanical Foundation of the Academy of Science of the Czech Republic:

Re: Request for specialist evaluation of submitted sample.

Dear Doctor Podlipský,

I am herewith submitting for expert verification the plant we discussed by telephone on August 25, 2002. Our other available sources have not ascertained anything concrete concerning this species. I am requesting an analysis be made without delay.

Many thanks,
A. Brom

The second letter is Podlipský's reply on August 28, 2002:

Dear Detective Brom,

First and foremost, the sample you submitted (parts of a flower and roots) was very likely the last such specimen of its kind. It is a great shame that you did not try to keep the plant alive, even though it would have been possible. For the world of contemporary botany it truly is a grievous loss. I cannot emphasize this enough. You should have immediately called a specialist and not acted rashly in such an unusual case. You cannot imagine the great damage your actions have caused.

Concerning your request: the plant does not officially have a name; it was withheld from classification. The topic of this semi-fabulous species (see below) was last briefly and tangentially discussed by a group of specialists in 1982 at an international conference in Tokyo, during which it was definitively concluded to be nothing more than a fabrication, an entirely unsubstantiated conjecture. It was not possible to reach any other conclusion. Until now, there was absolutely no evidence that would prove the existence of this flower, and this simple fact precluded any further debate.

I personally became aware of this "species" relatively late and quite by chance. During an internship in Kyoto twelve years ago, I was working on a lengthy article about intriguing extinct plants on the island of Honshu when I came across some information about the flower whose sample you

15

have just sent me. In the end, I made no mention of it in the article as I considered the flower then, given the nature of the information (I probably shouldn't call it information, obscure tales, rather), an invention, a botanical legend.

I first encountered the plant in an old collection of Asian stories from the early twentieth century that came into my hands during my Kyoto internship. The book contained a relatively comprehensive collection of Japanese legends, folk superstitions, strange incidents, and mysteries. Called a "kaidan," such stories dealing with inexplicable phenomena have always been popular in Japan — sometimes they are akin to fairy tales, but more often they have the character of a horror story. This was something similar. I read these stories in my free time for fun. One of them especially drew my attention because it, albeit marginally, was related to my field. It was a story about the flower Ushimitsuzoki (in translation: "Midnight"). It told of a lonely man who long ago cultivated a flower that would become the most faithful likeness of sadness. He called it Midnight. He invested all his resources into its breeding. The flower was marvelous, but could not survive long in the world and soon wilted. Because this flower was all he had, the man's sorrow led him to give his own life to it. He committed "seppuku" (samurai ritual suicide), and died with a wish addressed to the gods that his spirit be placed inside the flower. And indeed, not long after his death the flower thrived once again. In honor of this act, peculiar but romantic in the eyes of the era's high-born society, the flower became a supreme adornment for the upper echelons of the nobility.

I enjoyed the legend and wanted to find out whether this plant species actually existed, and if it did, I intended to mention this captivating story in my article. I tried to track down more information. I visited several archives, and finally, after a long and fruitless search, I succeeded in finding additional pieces of information in an ancient herbarium. The records were, in general, the work of laymen. As a point of interest, there were citations from the notes of a Japanese nobleman (I don't recall his name) from the 17th century (the beginning of the Edo period) who described the flower, now called Midnight. He said it was similar to a lotus flower, but generally much smaller and absolutely black . . . I remember that he used the comparison "like darkness," "like ink." The plant lacked any kind of leaf, only had long hair-like tendrils (exactly like your sample). I think it is important to note that this nobleman often described the plant as a "being" rather than a plant, as if it deserved its own special term of address.

The plant was indigenous only to Japan. It never grew freely in nature. It was artificially bred (reportedly as an ideal poison, it was later alleged to be employed for this purpose in Tokyo high society, which curiously contradicts the legend mentioned above). The entire interior of the plant is highly poisonous. Extracts from the flower could perhaps be used in small doses as a drug producing strong hallucinogenic effects, but nothing more specific was mentioned.

The Ushimitsuzoki flower was extremely rare. It was always only planted in small numbers. It was a very expensive "luxury" item. In some respects, the notes suggest, the plant conveyed social status, or, perhaps more accurately, ritualistic status. At one point it is spoken of as jewelry, a gem, or ornament, but again, no further explanation is given. Much remains unclear here, as if some facts were intentionally withheld for some reason.

So much for tales and legends. Regarding my present findings, I can say only this: in view of the plant's color and complete absence of any green surface, it most likely contains no chloroplasts, and therefore does not perform photosynthesis, i.e., it is most likely a type of parasite. But your assumption during our telephone conversation regarding its unusual method of nutrition can only be confirmed by thorough laboratory research. As the entire plant is fatally poisonous, there is the distinct possibility that Kryštof Warjak died from the poison contained in the plant. I will send you the results of my analysis for comparison as soon as possible.

For now everything else rests on primitive data and assumptions. You also mentioned some kind of thrusting movements the plant made when you discovered it. Could you send me a more detailed description? Would it be possible to meet to discuss it? I would be happy to go over some of the details.

In conclusion, a warning: it is certain that this flower would have a truly incalculable value for any informed private collector. I would recommend looking into the possibility that K. Warjak was trafficking in rare plants.

J. Podlipský

•

From the diary of Antonín Brom, page 23.

(undated)
The circumstances surrounding the discovery of Kryštof Warjak's body.

The discovery was reported on August 25, 2002, at 8:05 p.m. by Anna Bielinská. The body was first spotted by two children from a passing express train (international line, Prague-Wrocław): Petr and Štěpán Bielinský, sons of Anna Bielinská.

A. Bielinská told the train conductor she had seen what was probably a dead body lying near the tracks. At the next station the train stopped for ten minutes and Bielinská reported her sighting from the station telephone. They could not delay the train any longer. Bielinská and her sons were thoroughly questioned the following day in Wrocław.

We arrived on the scene at 9:20 p.m., an hour and fifteen minutes after receiving the call. According to Bielinská, the body was lying in a field of hogweed (an invasive plant that covers extensive areas in this region and is parasitic to former pastures and farmland) near the Polish border. We traveled to the site from the Těchonín train station on a handcar operated by two attendants. We slowly rode through the section of line corresponding to Bielinská's description. High walls of hogweed rose up on both sides of the track. We had no trouble recognizing the location. The first thing we saw was the red zippered sweatshirt on the dead body clearly visible in the vegetation.

Trains always brake on this section of track. As the train engineer later shared with me when questioned, this is due to the poor state of the track, which should be repaired in the near future. The autopsy allowed us to exclude the possibility that Kryštof Warjak fell from the train or was pushed off. It is likely he left the train intentionally. Why he did so remains unclear.

We cautiously entered the shadowy meadows netted with hogweed. The body was found not far from the tracks, about ten meters away. Plants wilted and blackened from some unknown cause lay inside a roughly three-meter radius around Warjak's body. They were partially covering the corpse. The whole place made an eerie impression. Unsettling. It was preternaturally tranquil. As if I had arrived in a sort of dead zone. Not a single thing was growing inside the circle. Everything had died. We noticed there were no insects in the zone, though whole swarms of mosquitoes were everywhere else in the humid, almost tropical air.

We realized this as soon as we arrived. It was already dark, so we lit up the area with handheld lanterns. After taking photos of everything, we were preparing to remove the plants obstructing our examination of the body when someone (maybe Lesný) suddenly noticed that moths attracted by the light did not approach the lanterns, as they would normally, but stayed at the exact distance of those three meters circumscribing the body. They did not venture beyond that border. It was not long before we were surrounded by an increasingly unnerving wall of buzzing insects drawn to the light and swarming at the line dividing living from dead hogweed.

Surprised and a little uneasy, we began by examining the area around the body. We took samples of shriveled plants and soil. Expert examination later revealed an unbelievable finding. Truly nothing was alive there. The dead hogweed had not rotted. No decomposition had occurred. And the soil contained no trace of any bacteria. Not even the smallest microscopic living organism was found. Death had stopped on a single spot, at a certain time, and it did not move from it. As if an anomaly in the ecosystem. At that moment our bodies were the only living things in that bizarre circle whose center was the dead Kryštof Warjak curled into the fetal position.

We inspected the body. Warjak lay curled on the ground, his head arched back and upward, his knees pressed to his chest. He was wearing a red sweatshirt, a T-shirt with a pale blue collar soaked with blood, corduroy trousers, and white tennis shoes. A hand covered his left hip, where there was a ten-centimeter-long wound, likely from a blade (the shirt was not torn around the area of the wound). As the autopsy revealed, the wound itself was not the cause of death. When I opened his stiffly clenched hand pressed onto his stomach, I saw that the wound had been unprofessionally sutured with a green thread, fourteen stitches poorly done and crooked, from which the blood found on the deceased's clothes must have leaked. We did not note any other external injuries. The autopsy provided more detailed information.

After documenting everything, we loaded the body onto the handcar and transported it from the Těchonín station to the hospital in Hradec Králové. When putting the body on the stretcher, we discovered it was attached to the soil by an unusual sort of filament, like a spiderweb. Later detailed analyses indicated that everything found in the area was permeated with intricate fibers of an unknown origin. Desiccated gray hairs. The body was no exception. It was literally veined with a dense network of these fibers.

●

It was evening after a rain. The earth flying past outside, undulating. Wind in the mouth. The sound and smell of metal everywhere. The zipper on a windbreaker clicking against the glass outside.

"Don't lean out so far," said a woman in the compartment.

The swift wind whipped the children's hair into each other's face. They laughed and screamed out the window, drunk on the rhythm of the iron wheels. The landscape rolled by like a strip of film, individual frames divided by the wooden columns of power lines. Rhythm. Beat. The pulsing of fields. The rhythm of soil and bushes. The rhythm of railroad buildings. Converging metal lines. Two shining fibers set into the landscape. Two fibers running to infinity.

The two boys glided their hands across the sky. Their palms shaped the wind, creating slits and vents between fingers. It was almost like touching something real, something alive.

Bells pealed at activated crossing arms. From the creeks and waterlogged meadows a chill rose into villages silenced by evening. The smell of oil at the small rural train stations they passed, sometimes cigarette smoke, and always the rainswept cracked cement panels of the train platforms, grass and low weeds overrunning the edges. At times they slowly passed the eyes of an unknown person standing on the platform, the gaze locked for a moment in that curious tunnel the color of human sclera.

A concrete ring colonized by brush in a field went by, a weir approaching an instant later. They were traveling along a branch of the river. Trees and shacks on the bank reflected off the water's surface. A fire of leaves and grass was burning in a garden. A fisherman in a small boat turned his head at the sound of the train pushing its way through the valley. For a second his eyes left the thin rings encircling the motionless fishing line sticking out of the river, the fiber uniting him with the world underwater.

The train slowed. It always slowed at this spot. The elder boy leaned out even further, contorted his lips, and spat. Both immediately pulled away from the window, laughing and jumping down onto their seats from the armrests they were standing on to lean outside.

The image of that evening, with all its smells and light, will forever be embedded somewhere deep in the minds of these two children. Whenever they recall it in later years, they will be overcome by a strange anxiety from something long ago, a tinge of nostalgia and a sense that they have irretrievably lost something precious. And they will probably never know that the mood of that ancient event, that forgotten journey through the borderlands, was exactly the same as one of the first childhood memories of the dead man the two children were just about to glimpse, in just a few minutes, lying curled up in a strangely overgrown patch of hogweed, and then point out to their mother with a simple "Mom, look . . . ," before their interest shifted back to observing in wonder the huge flowers swaying along the tracks. Flowers as tall as the train.

Yes, the very same memory was in the dead man, and everything the two boys now perceived from the compartment of the express train headed to Wrocław seemed a mere repetition of what he experienced long ago. He had smelled the wet earth of evening. He had breathed the same cool air the two boys were now breathing. He had watched the landscape streak past the train, and his eyes had flickered from side to side as if all the passing objects were catching his pupils and tugging, just as the boys' pupils were now being caught and tugged.

Everything repeats. Life begins at the first memory. The train slowed. It always slowed at this spot. With his every breath, his open mouth full of afternoon rain, the earliest memory the dead man bore within him was now being imprinted and etched into the two children leaning out the window of the express train slowly passing his body in a field of hogweed.

•

If we could retrieve the final thoughts coursing through Kryštof Warjak's dead brain, like extracting the last image reflected on a dead eye's retina, we would roughly discover the following:

He thought of Andrei. His childhood friend. The boy he had grown up with. Their lives intertwining forever after.

He thought of a flower. A single flower, a small plant that he mentally referred to as just "the flower," and it had become his life and he had become its life.

He thought of Nina. Andrei's wife. God knows why he recalled the fleeting movement of her hand brushing back a lock of hair fallen across her forehead.

He also thought of Kristýna, Andrei's four-year-old daughter, who had died at the end of May. She had inadvertently been poisoned from eating mushrooms.

He thought of Marián, his travel companion for a third of his life over a good portion of planet Earth. Together in the sultry air and warm soil of the tropical forest they had searched for all of those living stars, undoubtedly fallen from the heavens during a galactic event. The living remains of stars that had fallen into tropical forests and taken root in the soil, on vines, and in rotting wood. People then gave them a name. They endowed them with a word that precisely matched their appearance. *Orchid* . . . he had repeated that perfect sound, magnificent in and of itself, a million times in his life. Full of passion and desire.

He thought of the shadow. The entity who was always

somewhere right behind him these past days. Who had followed him on his journey all the way to this point, deep into old Europe, to the Polish border. Wherever Kryštof stepped, he could be sure HE would tread the same spot even before the imprint of his foot could fade from the carpet, that HE would touch the door handle or handrail in the subway before the heat of Kryštof's palm had dissipated. He didn't know his name. Maybe HE had no name. At times he had the feeling his pursuer didn't belong here. Here in this world.

He thought of his own body, which had somehow stopped sensing, of the world around him, which was suddenly not functioning as it should.

He thought of the small roots of vessels he felt in all his limbs when he concentrated, felt their every millimeter, saw them growing and twisting before his eyes, interweaving themselves amid the flickering in his tightly shut eyes.

•

Once long ago.

Kryštof ran over the footbridge across the creek. The metal construction quietly rang four times as his feet fell upon it. He noticed the sound of water flowing over rocks only when the dust of the field path once again hissed beneath his feet. His friend, Andrei, raced a short distance ahead of him. They passed the last house. It smelled of the black oil coating the shed and long fence. Kryštof ran his hand over its planks. The sun was low on the horizon and flashing between the slats, blinding him in the rhythm of the fence. He felt like laughing or shouting. He saw before him the stroboscopic, sun-punctuated, choppy movement of Andrei's thin frame.

"Come on," Andrei called over his shoulder.

They ran into the meadow. A swishing around them as the grass slid against their legs. Andrei blazed the path and Kryštof closed it behind him. Fluff and pollen flew into the air. The forest lay before them. Now evening, it seemed dark blue within. Even at a distance they could smell the sticky sap and hear its intermittent creak, as if someone were tuning an enormous musical instrument.

Andrei was fourteen years old, Kryštof two years younger. They had been friends since they were little. Kryštof didn't remember when they had first met. Whenever he came to the village, even after half a year, Andrei returned to his life with such ease it seemed they had never parted. Through Andrei he remembered everything, all the past years, the entire time he had spent there.

Kryštof had arrived with his mom the previous evening. She left him with his grandmother and grandfather for summer vacation. A vacuous vacation. This is what the word "vacation" always brought to mind. Countryside. Empty fields, meadows, and forest. The exact opposite of the city. He ran and breathed beneath the sky.

"What now?" Kryštof asked when they were in the forest.

"Let's go down to the creek."

Andrei kept on at a fast pace. They were out of breath passing the first pines. Kryštof stripped the bark from one along the way and crumbled it into small bits. He threw them to the side, strafing the tree trunks around them.

"Hey, it'll be dark soon," Kryštof stuttered insecurely. He quickened his step to catch up with Andrei.

"Well, you want to see it or not?" Andrei snapped at him. He was all tense. His irritation made him oblivious to the world around him. In his rush, he tripped over stones and roots sticking up in the path, stumbling with his hands thrust out in from of him, only a miracle kept him from falling. Andrei had been speaking in whispers about some secret of his since they had met up that morning. In a strange tone, unable to suppress a proud smile, he promised to show Kryštof something that evening.

They went down the slope to the creek. The forest around them had changed, grown shadowy. The lower they were, the more leafy trees there were blotting out the sky. Kryštof would have liked to turn around and go back to the village, but he was not about to admit it. Andrei adamantly struck his feet into the hillside. Stones and pieces of earth rolled down from his steps. He used his hands against the trees they passed to steady himself, not once looking back at Kryštof. A forest bird, startled by their presence, beat its wings nearby. The sound passed into Kryštof's chest and fluttered his heart. His pulse rose in his throat.

"How far is it?"

"We're almost there. Jesus, you afraid or what?" Andrei barked and went on silently digging his feet into the soft earth to keep from slipping. Kryštof was now very uneasy, stepping right behind Andrei into his plowed-up footprints, breathing the upturned earth (moist, the scent of mushrooms), his gaze trying to slow the approach of dusk above him.

They were down, in the ravine. They walked a ways along the creek. Andrei stopped and looked around warily. Kryštof was afraid. The promised secret tempted him no longer, he only wanted out of the forest. He was fed up with Andrei's entire demeanor, angry with him for how he had changed, hardened by an inner purpose, by something Kryštof did not understand. He didn't know Andrei like this. He suddenly seemed much older, more distant. He was also angry at himself for not turning back at the edge of the forest and returning to the warm, sun-drenched meadow. God knew what they could run into here. An animal could bite them, a stray dog with rabies, or something else.

Andrei bent down at one of the large rocks dotting the creek and surrounding slopes. He burrowed through the previous autumn's dry branches and leaves below it. He then crouched, lay on the ground, and sank his hand deep into the cool and dark hollow beneath the rock. He pulled out something about a meter long, wrapped in a plastic bag and tied with a string.

"Now watch," Andrei announced triumphantly, kneeling and unwinding the string from the plastic package.

It was a gun! Kryštof's eyes bulged.

A hunting rifle. He knew the type from his grandfather. It was always kept on top of the cupboard in the hallway so that he couldn't reach it. He was strictly forbidden to lay a finger on it. It always tempted him, attracted him, and naturally, on those rare occasions when no one was home, he would set a chair against the cupboard, place the largest pot from the kitchen upside down on top of that and, trembling with excitement, get a closer look at it, still not daring to touch it. His grandmother once told him about a boy who had shot off his sister's fingers and her entire hand when they were secretly playing with their father's rifle.

"Let me see it. Where'd you get this?" Kryštof asked. He momentarily forgot that the forest was now completely dark. He took a step toward Andrei, who just smiled.

Kryštof stretched out his hand, but Andrei did not give him the rifle.

"No way. You're still too little, you don't know how to use it."

That was a painful blow to Kryštof. He spun around, breathing quickly to drive away tears. He felt betrayed. Andrei had brought him out here only to demonstrate his superiority, to show how grown-up he was. That he wasn't a child anymore like him. Still, they always stuck together. Usually. When they weren't fighting about something.

"Shove it then!" screeched Kryštof, on the verge of tears. He turned around and began to clamber back up the slope. "I'll come back later and look at it anyway," he yelled over his shoulder.

"I'll hide it somewhere else," Andrei said coolly and continued to sit against the stone. Tears of anger gushed from Kryštof.

"I'll tell on you. You stole it!" he sobbed.

At that moment Andrei jumped up. Before Kryštof even finished turning around Andrei was standing behind him. Andrei threw him to the ground and shoved the muzzle of the gun into his back between his shoulder blades.

"Leave me alone!" Kryštof shouted. He propped himself up on one arm and tried to push Andrei away, shake loose of him, but he wasn't strong enough.

"You won't say a word!" Andrei laughed, and he pulled the trigger.

The creek flowed backward.

All the sounds of the forest went silent so that Kryštof could hear his teeth cracking, clenched against insanity. But he was sure the sound was in his body. That's how a breaking spine must sound. Crushed vertebrae torn from the body and driven deep into the dirt by a bullet.

He heard that cracking long after he realized the shot was a blank, the rifle wasn't loaded. Andrei laughed. It sounded somewhere far off and blended with the whistling and cracking in his head.

Weeping and sniffling, slipping and falling, Kryštof again started up the slope. Andrei called after him, telling him not to be stupid.

"Come back!" Kryštof heard behind him, "I'll totally let you borrow it." As if the words were not addressed to him, they flew around the surrounding slopes of the silent forest and then back down to the creek.

The sky was still blue, but lights were already on inside the village homes. Moist dew scented the grass. Andrei saw the outline of Kryštof's figure as it hurriedly crossed the bridge over the creek. Mosquitoes swarmed at the edge of the forest maddened by evening. Andrei walked slowly, running a hand over the meadow. The tips of plants tickled his palm. He had a strange feeling that something had ended between them. As if, for himself, he'd really shot him. In his existence.

Andrei stopped. He tore off a leaf of ribwort and for a moment sniffed its fibers. At first he was quite surprised that Kryštof had taken it like that. A stupid joke. Andrei couldn't resist the opportunity when he saw how scared Kryštof was. He didn't much care now. He only felt sorry that he had shown him the rifle in the first place. Kryštof might actually tell.

He'd definitely tell.

He felt strangely dirty (and somewhere in the corner of his conscience he felt guilty, though he wouldn't admit it). God knows why he remembered the time little frogs were born and the place was crawling with them (barriers of plastic bags were placed along the road to keep them from hopping into it), and they caught them and tied string to their legs and hung them on a tree like some weird living decorations, and then pelted them with a slingshot. He remembered they both had felt a mix of exhilaration and disgust long afterward at what they'd actually done.

Andrei took his time crossing the meadow. He tore at the grasses that got caught between his fingers, and, lost in thought, occasionally tasted the milk in the hollow of a stem. A bitter milk.

Kryštof told no one. When they asked him at home why he was crying and where he had been, he only said that he'd been in the forest and had a fight with Andrei. Grandmother, who'd never liked Andrei and was not happy that Kryštof tagged along after him, said everything would be fine, that he shouldn't worry about it, it was not the end of the world, or something along those lines, but Kryštof wasn't even listening. He ate his bread and soup, pulled the blanket all the way up to his chin, and as soon as the black plastic rotary light switch creaked and popped, he fell into a deep sleep.

From that day on, everything was different.

•

As a boy, Kryštof was afraid of plants. Huge poisonous herbs growing along creeks and paths. He sometimes came across hogweed in the village. There were a few places where it grew. He did not dare come any closer than twenty steps. He gave the plants a wide berth. Sometimes he threw stones at the hogweed from a safe distance. He would scoop up pebbles from the creek and, hiding behind a bush, chuck them at a monstrous stalk. Sometimes he managed to wound a plant.

Andrei once took him to the ruins of a deserted village densely overgrown with hogweed. He had never seen anything so terrifying. Andrei tried to convince him that hogweed once surrounded the whole village and no one escaped alive.

When Kryštof was in Prague and happened to see — in the courtyard, by the carpet rack, in a crack at the curb, or by the small sandbox in the park opposite their building — a shoot somewhat reminding him of hogweed, he would run home to grab a plastic bag, and with his hand protected beneath that thin layer uproot the sprout and toss it in the trash.

He was terrified that hogweed would invade the city. He imagined its roots tearing up the asphalt as it began to overtake city blocks and gradually grow into the buildings. Its caustic juices would menace people. The invasion would spread out from the river, where there was the most water. The plants would dislodge paving stones and rip up the riverbank to allow better access to the water. In time, the plants would close in around the last inhabited house.

When he was a little older, he soothed his fears with information. He tried to find out everything he could about hogweed. Every fact he discovered about the plants calmed him. The object of his fear was thus reintegrated into reality. It took a more solid form, giving him something to grasp. It was less agonizing to fear an actual plant than one created by a child's terrified imagination.

He became something of an expert. He knew the plant was commonly called Giant Hogweed. In Latin: *Heracleum mantegazzianum*. That other species of giant hogweed had been identified, such as *Heracleum sosnowskyi* and *Heracleum persicum*. That in Bohemia *Heracleum sphondylium*, or Common Hogweed, also grew and it sometimes crossbred with Giant Hogweed.

He read that *Heracleum mantegazzianum* could grow up to four meters high. Some sources claimed five meters. The stems of the largest specimens have diameters of over ten centimeters. Enormous flower blossoms could easily reach a meter in width. He memorized the organogenesis of hogweed: $K_5\ C_5\ A_5\ G(2)$ — this didn't give him anything to visualize, but it still reassured him to know it. The flowers are hermaphroditic. They are pollinated by insects. Even one solitary hogweed can produce seeds (twenty to thirty thousand of them).

Kryštof knew the plant had been introduced into Bohemia by sheer coincidence. Prince Metternich had hogweed planted in the park at Kynžvart Castle as an ornamental. The seeds were reportedly a gift to the prince from Tsar Alexander I at the Congress of

Vienna. It did not take long for the hogweed to escape the confines of the castle gardens.

In the Caucasus, the area of the plant's origin, hogweed is only half a meter high and generally unaggressive. It was purposefully cultivated to reach monstrous proportions. Only the most massive and stalwart specimens were selected for breeding, until a hulking monster slipped its bonds and spewed its seeds into open nature. We created the beast ourselves, Kryštof realized.

Giant Hogweed lost its natural enemies. It is inedible for the vast majority of animals. It became a strategic botanic assassin, systematically disseminating itself across the landscape. And it can grow practically anywhere. Invasion takes place along waterways, roads, and train tracks. The plant gradually sets up various positions to form a kind of epicenter from where it then begins a calculated eradication of competing species. It wages vegetal genocide. The battle over the moisture and nutrients of fertile ground. Hogweed learned to sprout remarkably early. In the depths of winter while other plants are resting in the soil. It sprouts and stretches its large, sharply jagged leaves out over the earth like a curtain against sunlight. In a short time the hogweed has formed an interwoven canopy that swallows up to eighty percent of the sunlight. Other plants are therefore unable to grow and starve to death.

Hogweed even created an effective weapon against animals. Its sap, the juice pulsing through its veins, is poisonous. It contains phototoxic substances. A compound that renders sunlight toxic. If someone gets hogweed sap on his skin, then sunlight becomes caustic. In the dark the person is safe, the skin is only mildly irritated, but once affected areas are hit by radiation, sunlight begins reacting with the chemicals contained in the sap and the skin is eaten away by the reaction and large painful blisters form that take a long, difficult time to heal. The skin in affected areas scars and changes pigment. It is enough for sensitive humans to merely inhale airborne particles of the plant or touch a leaf for them to experience nausea, runny eyes, burning in the throat, and other allergic reactions.

What Kryštof remembered above all was how hogweed could be eradicated. In terror he read articles from regional newspapers describing locations where a hogweed invasion had become a calamity, more often than not in northern and western Bohemia. In those places a fruitless battle had been waged for entire decades. They had tried all kinds of chemical sprays, an experimental approach to gradually habituate cows and sheep to the digesting of young hogweed that was not yet too toxic, manually cutting down full grown plants and digging up their massive roots (he recalled photos of figures in rubber suits with protective goggles and plexiglass visors with respirators to filter the toxic fumes emitted from cut plants). It truly did resemble a war. In some battle zones, the most intractable areas, specially equipped armored military transports were deployed. Metal tread crushed the horrific plants, and their reserve units sleeping in the roots were plowed up from the ground. And yet a year later new determined ranks rose up in the exact same places, carrying on the endless war over water and soil.

He learned that the most effective means of killing the plant was to inject it with a strong dose of herbicide directly into the stem. Kind of a low blow after all that cruel, albeit perfectly honorable, man (and sometimes machine) versus plant combat.

Kryštof learned many other things that helped him to transform the hogweed-phantom haunting him since his very first memory into a mortal hogweed plant. After an endless period of time, Kryštof was finally able to sleep in peace. He began pursuing interests like other children of his age. In time, his imagination found different objects to work with.

With all the knowledge he had amassed to dispel his fear, he was unconsciously preparing the ground for his later unbounded fascination with the world of plants. As he got older, his childhood fears retreated, embedding themselves in the most remote, secret corners of his mind, from where they would flicker only when something from the outside world struck him so acutely as to bring them to mind, and for a moment they would emerge from the mire of his unconscious into the light of his mundane life.

Kryštof grew up the moment he forgot about the plants that had once so filled him with dread.

•

As a boy, Kryštof rode the Prague-Wrocław line (maybe even on the same train as the two boys who first spotted his dead body lying by the tracks twenty-four years later) with his mother to visit his father in Poland. His parents lived far from one another for a time. Then they divorced. His father got a good position as an engineer in a steel mill in Katowice. It was supposed to be for two years, but he never came back.

Kryštof had no childhood memories of his father. All that stuck in his mind was that train journey. Hogweed. It was the first thing he remembered in his life. He stood on the armrest, watching the countryside after a rain scroll by, overgrown with the largest weeds in the world.

He grew up partly with his mother in Prague and partly in the village of his mother's parents. He later visited his father alone. Not to Katowice anymore, to Warsaw. He really only knew him from this meeting. As an old man, embittered by his empty life and all the alcohol he needed to drink every day.

His childhood was played out in these two worlds. It straddled the forest smells of the vast desolate countryside near the Polish border and the abyss of Smíchov tenement courtyards in Prague. Until he started school, he was almost always in the countryside. His mother did not remarry after the divorce. She went to work and didn't want Kryštof to spend so much time unattended. She decided to leave him with his grandparents for a while. In the beginning she tried to visit him every weekend. Gradually, the visits grew more sporadic. She had less and less time for him. He didn't mind much. He got used to it.

This long absence might be why he was never able to form a deeper relationship with his mother. As he grew up he hated her from the depths of his soul. They were always arguing. She also started drinking. At first only in the evening with the occasional bottle of wine in front of the TV. Then more frequently during the day. She always reeked of alcohol. She started having drastic mood swings and behaving erratically. He often found her passed out on the carpet or at the kitchen table. One severe argument ended with Kryštof telling her he'd find his own place with a friend. She didn't react. He took it to mean that she wanted him to go. He was sixteen.

He had problems at school. He repeated a year. He did poorly in math and physics. There was almost nothing he enjoyed. He was regularly tardy, smoked in the bathrooms, drew on the desks, got into fights, was rude to teachers, wrote his own letters of absence and forged the doctor's signature. He experienced the typical disgust at the abysmal idiocy and provincial need to be high-handed displayed by some of the teachers.

In his last year at school, he got a job in a Smíchov bar serving drinks, making coffee, and pouring beer. His shift was from six in the evening to one a.m. He began falling asleep in class. He finally graduated during the remedial period in September. He got three Ds and a B. He then worked off the books in a warehouse for a construction company. The only feeling he could later recall from that time was the persistent, steadily increasing hatred — although he managed to hide it — he quietly bore toward everything and everyone in that odd employment. He resented how insipid his warehouse coworkers were. Captive, he was subjected to their incessant discussions about football, hockey, cars, and the various parts of the female anatomy, the interminable recounting of the previous night's drinking, the never-ending drivel from television and tawdry color tabloids intended for that segment of the population with reduced cognitive faculties, and he observed the abiding pointless existence of all these people. He was forced to listen to the always playing radio, bucking up these creatures in their work. Commercial stations whose programming targeted an audience labeled as "rubberheads." It was as if these songs of impotent performers parasitizing the stupidity of their listeners were afflicting him like a disease.

He would return home absolutely exhausted and disgusted. Kryštof always clearly distanced himself from his surroundings. Not that he was blatantly anti-social, he just felt self-sufficient. And lonely. He had few friends. It took him a long time to open up to someone. Deeper relationships taxed him. He never stayed with a girl more than a few months. Always biding his time. He was looking for that one zest from long ago. And he never found it in the mouths of any of those girls.

As he gradually delved deeper into the mysterious world of plants, his solitude grew. He closed himself inside the biological rules of life and long growth periods. Time so different from human time. So serene. He sank into silence. One day he decided to conceal himself in that world forever.

•

A white cane his antenna, Pavel clattered his way over the paving stones. He did this more so that people would avoid him rather than from a need to probe his path. He oriented himself well. In the four years since the accident, since he'd lost his sight, his hearing had become so enhanced that on a "good day" (as he called it) the sounds and echoes bouncing off assorted materials, surfaces, and structures mapped out whole streets, rooms, or landscapes, whatever environment presently surrounded him. He even thought that through hearing he could visualize the faces of the people passing him on the street. He saw what those around him were wearing from the sound of their clothes rubbing. He even saw their gestures and reactions, all from the subtlest hiss of air set in motion. Since becoming blind, sound had become increasingly legible and recognizable, each sound distinguishing itself from another and accentuated.

He quite enjoyed this. Although he didn't much remember how the world used to look when he still had sight, his current state seemed much more colorful. Because his sense of smell had also become sharper and more powerful as his body sought new ways to grasp the things around him, he was suddenly able to recognize aromatic nuances that had once been hidden from him.

Pavel's problem was that he had lost enthusiasm for everything else. He observed how the people around him had turned into a sorry homogenous mass. After he became blind, his parents all at once decided to waste no time in making up for some imaginary emotional debt they thought they owed him. They were so solicitous and lavished him with such love that Pavel ended up feeling thoroughly revolted. The more everyone frantically tried to make clear that they were all the same, equals, the much more starkly he felt the opposite.

He found out at school that the teacher had distributed a flyer to the children with instructions on the proper way to behave toward the blind and how to assist them. From that time the relationship of the entire class with him became standardized. Everyone behaved as instructed. It was fun at first. Then it became unbelievably boring, as if he were sitting in a class of cloned children unctuous and cloying with kindness and understanding. He stopped speaking to them.

As his parents began to worry they became mushier and mushier until Pavel felt he was enveloped in a formless mud of touches and caresses, a compassionate, impeccably affectionate pap. He eventually lost the desire for any contact with people. He enjoyed listening to and smelling the world, but not speaking. Yet others pushed him into a corner. The more he needed peace, the more they tried to take it away from him. Words, words, words. He began to detest speech. Then one day he couldn't take it anymore. He lost patience.

He walked down a street composed of sound. Footsteps, glass, paving stones, the metronome at crosswalks, breathing, words, coughing . . . The constant, tedious brushing off of people who wanted to help him cross the street, get into the tram, get off the tram, walk up stairs, get hold of the railing, step onto the escalator. Constantly having to refuse seats vacated in the subway, always being alerted to oncoming cars, to holes in the street, to food kiosks he could already smell from around the corner, and, ultimately, to the curb, and so on.

He couldn't forget a dream he'd had the week before. He saw himself sleeping in his room. Behind the closed door was the silent apartment and darkness. He was sound asleep. Saliva shone in a corner of his mouth. Moonlight covered his face with the ornaments embroidered into the nylon curtains. He knew their shapes by touch. His fingers had often examined them while standing at the window listening to the soothing sounds of the apartment complex. They were spread across the carpet. The strange thing was that he could see all of it, as if his sight had returned. The window was ajar and behind it the distant city center quietly hummed.

The space between the prefab apartment blocks. A silent sandbox. Somewhere in it a forgotten plastic object. Motionless swings. The odor of cellars rising from the sleeping buildings. Extinguished housing estate. The moist aroma of concrete exhaled into the dreams of Prague's South City residents. Peace.

He suddenly saw one specific place in great detail. The concrete noise barrier stretching along the highway. When he was little and still had sight, he often played there. There were two ivy bushes growing in the shape of two figures. They looked as if they had wings. Leafy angels. Angels made from sickly city plants. He'd had such fantasies about them . . . They scared him . . . The children of the housing estate circulated all sorts of tales about them . . . Two phantoms were imprinted on that wall because they had failed to hide themselves underground before the sun came up. Their shadows remained like after an atomic explosion. The ivy then grew into the shapes of those shadows. Strangely, the bushes were not rooted in dirt, no part of them was in the ground . . . How could they live? On what? Maybe that's why the legend spread that the bushes detached themselves from the wall at night, unfurled their leafy wings, and flew off to suck water from the soft loam in the urban forest behind the housing estate. And they knew very well that water could also be found in people . . .

In the dream he heard the sound of leaves creeping into the room. Rustling like a treetop. He could still see himself asleep with those two ivy phantoms bending over him. Tiny filaments sprouted from his ears and nostrils. Bizarre white-green fibers the color of spoiled milk. He knew they were his hearing and smell. The phantoms reeled them in and flew from the room with his senses coiled into a ball. They soundlessly settled on the ground beside the sandbox and put down roots. Knitted to the thinnest roots, the milky threads of his senses were driven deep into the earth. It was painfully slow. The roots finally penetrated into an underground chamber. Someone there unwound the fibers of his senses from the roots and threw them into a huge cauldron. The cauldron boiled with guts, bones, and many things unrecognizable.

He was woken by his own screaming. The silence of the apartment blocks. Blindness. The partially open window admitted the faint drone of the city and the rustle of birch leaves stirred by the wind. He exhaled.

The next morning he left home and walked past the place where the two ivy plants grew. He stopped, the sun warmed his face. He felt out the ivy leaves with his white cane. Everything seemed normal.

He walked down a street composed of sound and scent. He was on Wenceslas Square. He walked uphill toward the National Museum. He had to. He had to go there every day. It was his shelter. Refuge. The only peaceful place in the giant grimace of city life. A quiet bubble in the migraine of the surrounding world.

He knew all the exhibits by heart. Every stuffed marten, seal, sparrow, bone of mammoth, and whale, and the likenesses of various extinct animals petrified in stone. He knew all the embryos suspended in alcohol, he saw them, how their crooked frog hands reached toward the walls of the bottles, how they opened their eyes black as newt spots. He also knew what no one but children saw. He sat and listened to what their parents told them in front of the display cases and what the children said to their parents. An incredible display of the most varied animals was assembled in his head merely from the conversations of museum visitors. He took a skeleton from the naïve world of children's questions and then wrapped it in the parents' expert explanations. The most bizarre creatures conceivable then came into being. He placed all these exhibits into glass cases throughout the halls and listened to the children admiring his ideas and imagination and pointing at them, but the parents did not see them and continued to instruct the children on how birds had neither gills nor teeth, and that snakes certainly didn't have tails, and that they should move on to the next display before another fraught discussion was triggered.

He had to be there every day. He didn't want to miss a single exhibit. His life was absolutely empty otherwise. He'd admitted it to himself once and tried to find what strength he could in it. He quickened his step.

Yet that day something was wrong. He poked ahead with his cane. Suddenly he smelled the guy. A homeless man with noxious vodka breath firmly grabbed his wrist. He was forced to stop. Before he could say anything, the man pressed into his hand some smooth papers. He guessed they were photos. He felt something warm inside him. Through his arm. In fear he tried to pry himself loose. Then there was nothing. He lost consciousness.

•

Andrei was from an orphanage. He didn't give it any thought until much later. At school they asked him why he said aunt and uncle instead of mom and dad, and then someone answered it was because he was adopted, a word he repeated to himself silently, and from that time on he felt somehow lonelier.

In the orphanage they remembered him as "Mister Crow." He was taken from his parents by the court as an abused and neglected child. When they brought him to the home he wouldn't speak with anyone. He only nodded or shook his head. He was afraid to be touched by an adult. When someone looked at him, he would cower in anticipation of the imminent blow, estimating movements and distances. He was small and emaciated. He screamed when they tried to bathe him, beating his tiny fists all around him, kicking and fighting. He was terrified of the water in the bathtub. He fought with the other children in the home, who laughed and teased him because he was different. He behaved strangely, not like the others. He was half Russian and spoke Czech poorly. He was five years old yet was still not toilet trained. His pants were always wet.

One day something snapped inside him. In the fenced yard behind the children's home they started throwing sand at him. It was late afternoon, almost dusk, children were playing in the sun-heated sandbox, Andrei was, as usual, on his own off to the side, digging with a small hoe.

Before he could shield himself, someone nailed him right in the eyes. The sand cut him under his eyelids. He stopped, covered his face, and, blind with fury, kicked sand in their direction. He apparently hit his target because as he was blinking and wiping the grains from his teary eyes someone lunged at him and tackled him to the ground, and then someone else knelt on him while the others around him shouted, "Let's give this asshole something to eat," as they took up handfuls of sand. Hearing that, a massive wave of hopelessness and despair welled up inside, and with an inconceivable burst of strength Andrei freed his left hand still clutching the little hoe from under a boy's knee and with all his might struck the boy and broke his collarbone. Only screaming followed. No one bothered him after that.

The staff didn't know what to do with him. Though hypersensitive and frightened, he also had a mean streak and was quick to anger. They tried to find a way to reach him. Andrei didn't need to speak, his forearm, shoulders, and back bore ten to fifteen small, dark spots of burn-scarred skin that spoke for him, enough that no one tried to get him to talk. Except for pain and fear, he had nothing to talk about. Those scars on the skin of this mean and rebellious boy kindled an abiding patience and compassion in the entire staff. When they glanced at that small constellation cauterized on his little arm by the burning cigarette his father would use to punish his misbehaving, they were incapable of scolding him.

They patiently dealt with his aggressive behavior toward the other children. They gradually taught him proper hygiene. Every month they increased the water in the tub he bathed in by one centimeter. They began with a puddle thumb-deep. Only cold water at first. Showering was out of the question. And no one could touch him when he was bathing or he would throw a tantrum.

The other children called the female staff "aunts" (Andrei did not address them at all). Children were divided into "families" of four or five. Each family comprised various ages of abused and neglected children and one caregiver living together in small institutional apartments that functioned like normal households.

Some of the children attended school, others were just beginning to walk or talk, while others had their diapers changed by staff and were bottle-fed. All of them lived together, and each child waited for the day their parents would show up to take them home. The staff knew that day would never come, but of course they never told the children and thought up other things to divert their attention. Of Andrei's relatives, the only one who showed any interest in him was a sort of grandmother once removed who, it seemed, lived in Russia. In St. Petersburg. Despite the distance and cost of postage, every Christmas she sent him a package of candy and toys.

At first Andrei was placed in a room of his own because the day after his arrival at the orphanage, when he was assigned to one of the "families," he had nearly strangled a girl to death for splashing him with water in the bathroom for fun.

The staff began to play a game with him called "Mister Crow." No one knows how it began. No one remembered anymore. Mister Crow may have been one of Andrei's distant relatives who someone had once mentioned. It may have been a white lie from the staff who were so desperate to establish communication they were ready to try anything. Or maybe it was Andrei, on the rare occasion when he spoke, who had called himself that . . .

In any case, "Mister Crow" became his alter ego. Surprisingly, his better one. He assumed two identities in relation to his surroundings. He was either the timid, silent, inaccessible, mean and aggressive Andrei, or the likewise timid and silent yet now polite, gentle, at times even friendly Mister Crow. It depended on how someone spoke to him. It was quite simple. Usually it was enough to say: "Mister Crow, be a good boy and make your bed," or "Mister Crow, it's time to brush your teeth!" or sometimes, "Mister Crow, if you bite Alena one more time, you will go kneel in the corner!"

Only in this way could Andrei release his past. Andrei had experienced dark things. He had eaten from the dog's bowl, been burned with cigarettes, and nearly drowned in the bath. Whereas Mister Crow was a stranger who had nothing in common with Andrei, that is, besides the body they shared. Mister Crow had a desire to live, to discover the world, which was perhaps not as malevolent as it had originally appeared. Andrei was resigned, losing orientation and certainty. The crack beneath his feet was speeding with an icy screech toward the shore. He was afraid to move. Rather than taking a false step, he froze up and waited. Below him fish were suffocating, and it was bitterly cold.

Everyone liked Mister Crow more. Soon the children were calling him that, too, and gradually they began to get along better. In time he completely fell into the collective. He eventually overcame most of the ingrained fears and habits caused by the neglect and poor upbringing he had received as a child. Someone even saw him laugh once. Truly a great event.

In the end one of the caregivers, Mrs. Březinková, decided to take Andrei into foster care. She had just left the orphanage after three years of such work had emotionally drained her. So Andrei got a new family who provided him with a forgotten feeling of security and surrounded him with love, which he absorbed like soil does water. First this love had to slowly and laboriously dissolve the hard, crusted husk on the surface of his soul, before Andrei would warily allow it, many months later, to enter him. Mister Crow was now completely forgotten. Andrei was again whole, a unified personality. In time the scar from the previous division healed and almost disappeared completely. He became Andrei Březinka.

•

From the diary of Antonín Brom, page 41.

August 28, 2002

On the basis of the evidence collected, Kryštof Warjak trafficked in plants. Over the past eight years he visited Thailand once, Malaysia twice, Bolivia twice, Peru once, Brazil three times, and Venezuela once. How he acquired the money to fly to these destinations is not known. He had no documented employment for a whole decade. The employment office has no record of him. He received no unemployment benefits. He never submitted a single tax return. Only his health insurance was properly filed. Before each departure to one of the previously mentioned countries in Asia or South America he spent a substantial sum of money on inoculations and anti-malarials. He also paid fourteen thousand crowns a month in rent for an apartment in Prague 3.

In the apartment of Warjak's colleague Marián Rotko (where Rotko was found dead August 27, 2002), twelve strictly protected and endangered species of orchid were discovered, whose value (i.e., the price they could be sold for on the black market) has not yet been determined, but according to the initial estimates of experts, it would definitely be in the hundreds of thousands of crowns.

Warjak intended to sell the plant he was transporting to an unidentified collector. Based on all available information to date, probably someone from Russia. We currently know of three contacts/connections (Khalkin, Styepanov, Bardyaev), each in a different European city where Warjak could deliver the plant. The delivery points were Vienna, Prague, and Wrocław. Khalkin and Styepanov were violently murdered. Bardyaev has been arrested and hospitalized in critical condition.

•

Kryštof got into plants thanks to a part-time job he found one summer while still in high school. Every afternoon he would ride through the scorching city by tram to the Košíře district to water an old man's garden.

That summer was particularly scorching. The dog days lingered in the city, and Kryštof, who had never understood that phrase before, could now imagine a giant, invisible hound skulking through the streets, drinking from puddles of warm air on the roads, licking everyone's foreheads and underarms with its sticky tongue, and its searing breath filling public transportation and every crevice and hollow beneath the clothes of passengers. Its breath reeked of melted ice cream, spilled beer drying in the sun, cigarette smoke, and sounded like a trash can full of wasps gnawing away at bits of plastic. Just a faint rustling and wheezing. It was impossible to escape.

Evenings brought little relief. They were humid and lay heavily on Prague with all its warm tiles, bricks, and paving stones. Passing through the city after sundown would find a rather uncommon lively atmosphere. Windows were open onto the streets and court-yards so that one could continually hear the sounds of apartment life. Everything coalesced. Discussions between father and son, the screams of children, an old man's laugh, a woman sobbing in her kitchen (tears pattering wetly onto unwashed dishes), the moans of lovers, a machine gun firing from a television, the clamor of a party, a brass band clanging like an overturned cupboard full of glass and cutlery. The sounds of the night wove together and created an ineffable commotion that lent the city a touch of peculiar luxuri-ance. Heat inflated life. As if everyone was overcome by a delirium from the heat pervading the deepest recesses of their bodies that had for so long retained cold.

Days passed, and every afternoon at six o'clock Kryštof observed the heat-altered city from the tram. The sun ran along with him, pouring itself onto one tenement window after another. It slid along open glass doors and shop windows. It glared from door handles, necklaces, earrings, and belt buckles, it dully slid down the sweaty backs of Ukrainian workers in a ditch before immediately leaping onto the sunglasses of a woman standing at a tram stop, from where it moved to the collar around a dog's neck, shining almost imper-ceptibly in the saliva of the dog's hot dangling tongue, then slid down the crutches propping up an old man and onto the plexiglass covering the tram schedule atop its post. It disappeared for a moment behind a tall building, but suddenly fell back again onto the steel tracks and in no time covered the windshield of an oncoming tram, and on and on in this way as if a secret relay race of light passed between people and things.

From the stop where he got off the tram, Kryštof had to walk a short distance uphill. Bathed in sweat, he trudged through a neighborhood of villas. Along the way he inspected the homes. Old houses with peeling façades, covered in ivy, plunged into the shadows of tall trees. Peace and quiet like somewhere in the countryside, with only the occasional tram scraping around a bend below.

The old man's name was Živný, meaning nutrient. He lived alone in a large house built into the slope at the turn of the century. A spacious garden surrounded the house and was separated from the outer world by a high brick wall with a single rusty gate. It was this garden that in time revealed to Kryštof the secret beauty hidden in the world of plants, and if someone ever succumbed to it, his remaining days would be enshrouded in fog like a tropical fever.

At first he only tended to the outdoor flowers and bushes. After seven o'clock, when the sun no longer burned and the heat of the day turned into a sultry airlessness, the water was able to stay in the soil longer (otherwise the sun's piercing rays would pull it right up into the sky). He filled a tin watering can to the brim at the well in the corner of the garden and began making his rounds of the footpaths and broken tiled walkways between the beds and trees. He watered a wide variety of flowers, some familiar and others completely unknown to him. Exotic creepers clambered up the weathered façade of the house. Beds of tulips and roses thirstily stretched toward the spout of the watering can. He walked along the fence where bushes of decorative rosehip, magnolia, and rhododendron were planted.

He changed hands often. The water hollowly splashed in the can. Every time he walked from the well with a full can of water, its overflowing rose dribbled onto the concrete steps. His tennis shoes were always soaked when he was finished.

Živný was a rather eccentric old man. He looked to be around eighty. He walked hunched over, his back completely crooked and his legs bowed, his whole body moving in a rickety fashion amply assisted by the inanimate limb of his cane. Yet he was unbelievably vital. His steady hands possessed a powerful grip, and his lively and sharp eyes darted relentlessly over everything around him.

Kryštof could not stand him for the first month. Živný was always breathing down his neck, instructing and admonishing, chiding him either for under-watering or over-watering. ("You'll make it rot!" he'd lose his temper and yank the can from Kryštof's hands.) He was always going on about something. He was surly as all. He didn't care much for people and hated animals. When any of the neighborhood cats wandered into his garden, he shot at them with a slingshot. He was even known to use it on children. The neighborhood took him for a lunatic. He hated all of society and was forever fulminating against politicians, businessmen, the police, artists, the bureaucracy, young people, old people, the whole "rabble," as he summarily lumped everyone together. He had no television, only read newspapers, usually several weeks old, which he pilfered from the recycled paper dumpster.

Even though he didn't drink, he looked absolutely plastered most of the time. He never reeked of alcohol. At first Kryštof thought he must be on pain medication because Živný occasionally mentioned that he had to go for a checkup. To be more precise: "Those idiots at the hospital dragged me in again yesterday for another useless exam."

Živný also lied and fabricated liberally. He once told Kryštof how he and his wife, when she was still alive and they were both young and in love, took a trip to Italy for two weeks and were lucky enough to see in Naples the famous collection of this or that flower collector because it was being exhibited at the time. He described the Italian countryside, the difference between the southern and northern regions, the warmhearted nature of the inhabitants, told stories from their trip, and went on at length about wandering around Rome — and then not one hour later he'd claim he never married because all the women he'd ever met were greedy, calculating bitches, and he would never stick his nose outside of Prague because the local boors were enough for him and he had no need to see for himself that a smack was the same as a slap no matter where you went. And then a short time later he would be upset about how Aněžka and Josef (his supposed children) were neglecting him, how they hadn't come to visit him in such a long time, after he had given them life and lovingly raised them, and how they didn't bring him any joy and never brought his grandchildren to see him. After that he would launch into a long-winded reminiscence of the end of the war in forty-five, how the Germans were fleeing the Russians and trying to be captured by the Americans, how he and his mother hid in the cellar and he peeked outside at his father trying to calm a German soldier who was shouting that the Czechs had to be shot because if not they'd start shooting Germans, when grenade shrapnel suddenly ricocheted into the cellar and hit him in the groin, and then how he had to be operated on for ten hours and they saved his life in the hospital but couldn't save his manhood, so he was sterilized, and — he added — that had liberated him from all the inanity of love and similar such amusements for beasts and imbeciles.

He once told Kryštof of the apparent cause of his illness. He said he'd never be cured because no one really knew what was wrong with him. They continued to call him in for examinations because his illness, they said, was an unknown phenomenon. A whole team of doctors had been observing him for thirty years and had come up with nothing. He said it had happened a long time ago when he was returning from a friend's funeral. It was July and a horrible heat wave was baking the countryside, just like this summer. He was walking in that terrible noon inferno on a path between fields when, out of the blazing blue, a hailstone fell right into the barley. An inexplicable phenomenon. A single hailstone big as his fist. He said no one believed him because he had no proof. Well, given the heat and how drained he felt, he picked up the hailstone and drank it, the whole thing. He swallowed every drop of water as it melted. It was ice cold. That evening he came down with a fever and inflammation or something. No one knew what was wrong with him. He felt unbearable pain in his stomach. The fever lasted a month. He said he never got rid of the pain.

"That's how it was and that's how it is!" Živný suddenly shouted out as if Kryštof were disagreeing with him. He had said nothing, only listened and nodded to indicate he was paying attention. "No one believes me!" he shouted. "You're all the same! You think I don't see you laughing at me? Cretins!" he barked over his shoulder and limped off offended.

A large greenhouse stood in the corner of the garden. At first it was strictly off limits to Kryštof. The first summer he came only to water the garden. Živný would not even allow him to peep through the glass. Summer swung into autumn, work started to dry up in the garden, and Živný told Kryštof that he was no longer needed and he would call if something changed. But nothing happened, and Kryštof assumed his work there was over. Not that it mattered much, he told himself, the pay wasn't particularly good, Živný was a freak, and so on. But it had grown on him. Something was drawing him back. He had come to like the quiet old garden, which must have been enchanted in some way. Nowhere else did he experience the same feeling of the frozen time sprawled there, encircled by the crumbling brick wall.

He liked all its strange corners. The old footpaths leading to the black shed, locked with a chain, the lock so rusty no one was able to open it anymore. What could be inside? The odor of wheel grease and kerosene, loads of tea and cacao cans filled with rusty screws and nails. An ancient, smoothed workbench covered in screwdrivers and chisels of various sizes. A vice. Assorted plastic bottles of oil and solvent, a canister of lubricant. A blanket of sawdust on the floor. Strips of light in the cracks between the boards. Dead spiders hanging in still, forty-year-old webs.

And other paths and walkways leading uphill to the greenhouse, just as inaccessible and mysterious. A muted green color shone through the sweaty glass. In places a leaf would touch the moist pane. It looked as if it were suffocating and pleading, pressing its hand on the glass to be released into the air.

He had even begun to enjoy the old coot's endless stream of fabrications as they became ever more fantastic and crazy. He told stories from the war, about how he had taken part in the Prague Uprising in May 1945. He claimed he had fought on Troja Bridge and in Stromovka Park, then his unit moved to the radio station because they were continually broadcasting calls for help. He recalled how they had built barricades from overturned tram cars and paving stones and how during the battle of the radio building he had fired a panzerfaust at an oncoming tank, disabling its gun, and half-suffocated Germans jumped out and were shot at like rabbits. Živný colorfully described how on the ninth of May the mob hanged collaborators from the streetlights, and Germans who had not managed to escape were burned alive. He then told of his experiences from the First World War and remembered Emperor Josef, how everything had been better in his time and that today everyone was rushing headlong to their doom because they didn't know how to live anymore, they would rather stare at the television. He then said he was arrested by the StB, the secret police, because someone had reported that he was threatening to blow up his neighbors at night in their sleep with dynamite all ready to go in his cellar. "Obviously those bastards were cooking up a way to move me out of here!" he shook a fist over the fence at his neighbor's windows.

And Kryštof enjoyed observing the slow life cycle of plants. Their peculiar way of cohabiting in this world. In it he found his own form of inner peace. He was absolutely disgusted by what was happening beyond the borders of this garden world, all the responsibilities outside, constant worries, coming up with the rent on time (his father did send him money on occasion, but only enough to cover the hole in his rarely sober conscience), his mother's descent into alcoholism, and the insecurity of his own future in all of that misery. As time went on, this is where he ran to forget.

So he was glad when Živný called in the spring and, overflowing with insults and outrage toward doctors, informed him that he would undergo surgery at the end of May and would be bedridden for at least two weeks "in that lice-infested hospital." Then in a hushed toned he said that their real intention was to dismantle him for organs and transplant them into young athletes on a waiting list, that it was the biggest business in the world.

While Živný was laid up in Motol Hospital, Kryštof had to look after everything in the house and the garden. Including the greenhouse. He was giddy with excitement. When the old man first brought him inside, Kryštof knew this was the place. This was his destiny. All those orchids and other various botanical complexities in the humidity and heat resembling a rainforest. It swallowed him and shut him inside forever. The greenhouse felt like a womb. The safety of a warm, wet world where the only law and principle was life. Endless forms and expressions of life. A lushness he had never before seen anywhere. As if all those flowers, through their constitution and through the whole of their bodies, strove with a fierce determination and an unremitting painful desire straining within to utter the name of God.

Živný explained and demonstrated everything that needed to be done. Each plant required its own special care and regimen. Now he was grumpier than ever. Kryštof was only able to bear his insults and constant griping by envisioning himself soon being alone among all those flowers.

He demanded that Kryštof endlessly recite the exact procedures for fertilizer use and watering for every individual species. When he messed up or forgot something, the old man whacked him with his cane and roared that he had never seen such a moron in all his lifelong days. He would get so upset at times that he went red all over and had to sit down for a moment to catch his breath. Kryštof was afraid Živný would hurt himself like this because he wheezed for his life and clutched at his heart. Each time Kryštof comforted him, apologized, and calmed him down, usually while receiving blows from the cane and the old man's furious imprecations that Kryštof obviously wanted to give him a heart attack so he could then rob him.

Things continued this way for about two weeks. Finally the day came when Živný left for the hospital. It was a cool but sunny early evening. A slight breeze was blowing the air clean, and it tasted like somewhere by the sea. It was easy to breathe. Kryštof was sitting by the greenhouse observing the scars airplanes left in the sky. Živný was different this time. He had become a slumped old man, bent under the heavy sadness of his existence. He walked through the garden and said goodbye to everything. He touched the flowers as he passed them, crumbling their pollen in his fingers and sniffing them. He was suddenly tired, all his vigor gone. Queerly reticent, he shuffled along the wall bewildered. He paused and waved his hand in the air to remove a spiderweb hanging above the path between bushes. He did not want it sticking to his face or the Sunday suit he was wearing to go to the hospital. To Kryštof, observing him from afar, it seemed that Živný's airy wave was to ward off death.

When they said goodbye at the gate, the old man laughed and patted Kryštof on the shoulder. That was the last time he saw Živný.

•

He opened his eyes. Rain howled on the other side of the curtains. Dawn had not yet broken. Absolute darkness. The room smelled of plaster and starched sheets. A hardened bar of cheap soap in the bathroom. Water leaked from under a peeled patch of wallpaper above him. It dripped onto the blanket covering him. The fresh moisture seeping through watered the dry flower that had blossomed on the ceiling during the previous rainy period. It blossomed from the rotten plaster. A huge gypsum orchid full of poison. Its dark brown printed petals were coming unstuck from the wall and, moving like a child opening a hand in his mother's body, unfurling into an enormous flower the color of a water stain. The air in the room was so damp from it that even the lump of soap in the bathroom had dissolved, and with each breath he took its acrid odor clogged his pulmonary alveoli. Now he expected the first flower petal to touch his face at any moment.

An unceasing downpour in the morning sky over the dirty streets of a foreign city. He silenced the electronic beeping on the nightstand. He was now holding four digital numbers encased in plastic. There's still time. He hit snooze for five minutes. He closed his eyes again. He recalled a trip he took along the Baltic Coast. The shades of that coast provided a needed salve to his tired and sleepless eyes. A place out of season. A snow-covered beach. Mica crystals glittered in the plaster of houses and frost in the air. He traveled through deserted tourist resorts. He slept in empty hotels and rooming houses. Wooden hangers clattered in the wardrobes and everything smelled like plywood and cheap soap. This is a place I could see myself living one day, he thought. The Baltic.

The alarm rang again. He peered into the darkness. Outside the window was a ledge and rain.

They had twenty-five days for their trip through the rainforest. A meet-up with Marián in two days. He arrived in Puerto Maldonado the night before. A marathon flight with layovers in Madrid and Lima. Now he needed to get to Sandoval, then maybe take a local car. He had some tenuous contacts . . . He'd have to see about that . . . More importantly, he had to find a good guide . . .

The rainy season. Rain began every afternoon at five. It did not let up until an hour after daybreak. He did not feel up to it this time around. Wet. Everywhere. He was confused and exhausted from jet lag. It always took him at least three days to adjust. All the chemical ills of anti-malarial tablets he'd started taking a week before his departure coursed through his blood. He always coped poorly with prophylaxis. Damned Lariam . . . The side effects of the pills might have been worse than the malaria itself. For his previous trips he had already been inoculated against yellow fever, every kind of hepatitis, diphtheria, rabies, typhus, and the other sought-after tourist delights of South America. He began hallucinating after a couple days of taking the Lariam. Horrifying nightmares woke him. He had recurring dreams about death. He suffered from excruciating stomach pains. He often woke more exhausted than when he had fallen asleep . . .

He stood up in the cold puddles on the floor and warmed himself by spewing out the most foul invectives he could muster. He resolved not to save money on accommodation next time. Water dripped from the ceiling in several places. He threw back the curtains. The sky was beginning to lighten. The wall of rain droned on like a sluice. Aside from the cross on the wall, the nightstand, bed, and a single chair, the room was completely bare.

He slipped into pants and sleeves. He pulled on solid leather boots. He put on a rubberized jacket made of permeable spacesuit material. He practiced putting on his backpack, jumping a couple times, and walking back and forth across the room. He then took it off, opened it, took out a small tank of gas, regrouped several items, and returned them to the pack. He closed it and fastened the straps and buckles.

Flowers are the most complicated forms of beauty
orchids growing from rotting wood
into humid tropical air
are like small explosions
orchids are the jungle's soft spots
orchids opening their mouths in forbidden reaches of the forest
smelling as no other flowers can
smelling like the tongue of a sixteen-year-old girl
plants so reminiscent of a woman
so elemental and sensual

that young Brazilian Indians secretly love them
rain breaks onto naked boys' backs
rain envelops and conceals them
they seek out only those most like female genitalia
their eyelids quiver
with hot breath they seek a path in flower petals
then drunk on all the sultry amorous pollen
they rape their flowers

Sticky lashes of carnivorous sundews
they chastely conceal the blind eyes of the plants
they fall asleep with a fly beneath their lids
silently dreaming their hungry dreams
and guarding these boys' secret

A trail runs on the surface of a river
the forest looks like a biological alphabet
that is impossible to read
the ancient calligraphy of the tropics
the ancient letters of decay and rebirth
in a daydream
through the chink between the massive inhale and exhale
of the jungle
they slip inside unobserved

Day breaks
everything is in warm mist
they wade across a stream
their clothing weighed them down
Kryštof watches the guide's back
an Indian boy

with bones beneath brown skin
who sometimes looks back at him with animal eyes
swinging in his gait as if floating
bending under vines reaching into the path
opening the rainforest with a long knife

•

From the diary of Antonín Brom, page 45.

August 29, 2002

It has been verified that the thirty-year-old man found dead on August 20, 2002, in the Marilyn Monroe Pension, near a highway exit on the northern edge of Vienna, was there to receive a plant from Kryštof Warjak. In all likelihood he is Nikolai Alexeyevich Khalkin, with a record for drug trafficking in Russia. His identity has still not been definitively confirmed.

Suspected of his murder is Simon Baumgarten, a fifty-six-year-old Viennese vagrant, currently in custody pending investigation. He was arrested on the basis of a statement given by the night receptionist of the Marilyn Monroe Pension.

Baumgarten arrived on August 19 around eleven p.m. According to the receptionist, he was wearing a blue and white windbreaker, stank of sweat, was unshaven, his face red and swollen, and generally did not inspire much trust. The only items he had on his person were a plastic bottle of Coca-Cola and a handheld video camera (a cheap one, but still suspicious in view of his repulsive appearance). He introduced himself to the receptionist as Warjak and requested that she call Khalkin's room and inform him that he had a guest, which she reluctantly did. Khalkin surprisingly told her to send him up. The receptionist knows nothing about what happened in the room. In any case, after three and a half hours, Baumgarten left the pension and Khalkin was found by the maid the following morning with his throat cut.

Baumgarten killed Khalkin with the bottle of Coca-Cola. In the room Khalkin's body was found, there was also the video camera Baumgarten had brought with him (his fingerprints are all over the device). Inside was a recording of Khalkin's death. From the recording it is clear that Baumgarten was holding the camera. The murder lasted a few hours. Baumgarten switched on the camera and held it pointed at Khalkin. He did not move the shot from his face the whole time, so we don't exactly know what Baumgarten was doing, but it could be conjectured that he was somehow holding Khalkin in check. (Was he pointing a gun at him? We have no way of knowing. If yes, it likely did not have a silencer because he otherwise could have used it as the murder weapon.) Baumgarten is not seen during the entire recording, only heard speaking to Khalkin.

It was immediately evident from the video that Khalkin's left arm was broken as he was holding it at an unnatural, disjointed angle down across his body. He looked roughed up (a bloody lip, a welt under his eye). He was sitting by the nightstand with a swollen mouth holding something inside it, and breathing in terror. He had a pen and paper in front of him. From the left side of the room, Baumgarten ordered him in English (although after his arrest Baumgarten claimed and still claims he doesn't know English) to write on the paper the current location of Kryštof Warjak and the reason why he did not take the planned flight from Tokyo. Khalkin wrote something quickly and emphatically — it is not clearly visible in the video, but I assume he wrote that he didn't know. Baumgarten then told him he had three hours to remember. He was also to write down names. Names of the others, their locations, telephone numbers, and any other information concerning Warjak, flowers, and anything else related to them. He promised that if Khalkin remembered within three hours without swallowing once, he would let him live. Khalkin started to cry, as much as he could with a swollen mouth. He *sniveled and whined. The following hours of the recording were exactly the same. Khalkin walked around the room, sometimes sat down and then got up again, he was extremely nervous, his face increasingly puffy, and his eyes avoided the relentless lens of the camera. He did not swallow. He then wrote on the paper for about five minutes.*

After thirty minutes more he sank to his knees. His entire face was contorted. He writhed in pain. He lay on the floor and howled. Baumgarten said in his raspy voice that he was still missing the information about Warjak and set the same pen and paper on the ground beside the groaning Khalkin (here Baumgarten's hand appears this one time). Khalkin, face wrenched in pain, wrote something quickly and shakily. Baumgarten took the paper and said calmly: "That is obviously nonsense, don't think it will be so easy for you to lie your way out of this. Your efforts are now completely useless."

At the two hour-and-forty-three minute mark of the recording (displayed in the bottom corner of the screen) Khalkin opened his mouth and sobbed as Coca-Cola spilled from his lips. All his teeth, his tongue, and parts of his gums had dissolved in it. At that moment, Baumgarten set the camera on the nightstand and pointed it toward the wall (where it was later found untouched). Then we only hear Khalkin's attempt at a scream, but it's actually a loud hoarse hiss as his vocal cords were likely gone at this point. Then only gurgling as he died. Water in the bathroom (Baumgarten probably washing his hands). Finally, the door slamming shut. The recording continued for three more hours in its fixed view of the wallpaper. Baumgarten killed Khalkin silently with a thin strip of plastic cut from the bottle of Coca-Cola.

So much for the circumstances of the murder. In his statement, Baumgarten denies ever being in the pension, although his fingerprints in Khalkin's room and voice analysis from the video recording unmistakably identify him. He claims he has never heard the names Khalkin,

Warjak, Styepanov, or Bardyaev, and insists he suffered several days of amnesia.

Simon Baumgarten was arrested on August 22, 2002, (shortly after 1 a.m.) in Prague. It is not clear how he got here. He was found on National Avenue with an open fracture in his shoulder, suffering from hypothermia and heavy blood loss, completely exhausted and disoriented (he only spoke German). Many witnesses corroborated the same.

One important connection (discovered only in the advanced stages of investigating the Warjak case) is that on August 21, Marián Rotko, Kryštof Warjak's associate, was attacked on the street by a vagrant. Police making their routine patrol at around 9:45 p.m. saw Rotko unexpectedly tackled to the ground and then subdued by his attacker. Rotko's description, given at the scene, corresponded exactly to Baumgarten: an older man in a dirty nylon jacket, red splotches on his face, etc. When the patrol car stopped, the attacker (Baumgarten) was kneeling on Rotko and probably trying to rob him (Rotko stated that he did not know what the attacker wanted). When Baumgarten saw the police, he released Rotko and fled. The police were not able to apprehend him.

Although it seems impossible and preposterous, Baumgarten crawled into a subway ventilation shaft (an opening about 34 cm in diameter). Officer Martin Koutský reported that the attacker intentionally injured himself by dislocating his shoulder in order to crawl through the shaft (!). This seems quite unlikely in view of the fact that the injuries requiring Baumgarten's hospitalization were more serious in nature (torn shoulder muscle, shattered bone). It is possible he sustained the injuries during his escape from Koutský (though it is not clear when or how) or while in the subway ventilation shaft. Koutský sensibly determined that Baumgarten could not survive in the shaft and called in a team to search for his body. The search was called off two and a half hours later when Baumgarten was found at the National Avenue subway station.

Simon Baumgarten is now recovering from his operations. I have conducted the initial interrogation. I have certain suspicions (which can be confirmed or refuted on the basis of a thorough psychiatric examination) that Baumgarten truly experienced a strange form of amnesia. Medical personnel have reported that when the anesthesia wore off, Baumgarten woke up totally confused and disoriented, spoke only German, stuttered, and refused to accept that he was in Prague. He insisted he was in Vienna. That he fell asleep or passed out in a park near Vienna's Hauptbahnhof and remembers nothing since that time. He says he woke up in the arms of some man.

According to eyewitnesses, the situation transpired as follows: Baumgarten broke through the glass doors of the closed National Avenue subway station, walked into the street without stopping or minding his surroundings, likely in shock from his injuries, and then slipped out of someone's grasp as they tried to get him to sit down (it was apparent Baumgarten was about to collapse). Witnesses report that his face was twisted in pain as he approached a drunk beggar sitting by the entrance of the Tesco department store (where the homeless and drug addicts often spend the night) and collapsed into his arms. Witness Petr Kalina was waiting for a tram and saw the entire event: the drunk vagrant rifled through Baumgarten's pockets with no regard for his injuries or general physical condition. He took some photographs and papers from Baumgarten and then shoved him away in disgust. He got up to leave, which Kalina tried to prevent, but obviously could not.

•

Kryštof was a flower smuggler. A trafficker in biomass that people considered beautiful. A trafficker in cellular explosions frozen in time. He traded in flowers the ancient Greeks called Aphrodite's Sandal. He traded in flowers delicate as snow.

He worked for three weeks, at most a month, out of the year.

Every so often he would fly to Peru, Brazil, Bolivia, Venezuela, Malaysia . . . anywhere in Asia or South America that contained a tropical rainforest.

He would then wander the jungle for a couple of weeks looking for flowers. Only rare and critically endangered species. Internationally protected plants whose poaching was punishable by hundreds of thousands of dollars in fines and several years in prison.

Trade in endangered flowers is one of the most marginal and least known areas of the black market. Large sums of money are involved because the buyers always belong to the upper echelons of society. With the right contacts it is relatively easy to become immersed in this demimonde. Anyone with any kind of access to the desired commodities automatically becomes an organ in the immense and secret body of plant trafficking. Private collectors and officially non-existent representatives of high-end cosmetics companies (who use prohibited flowers to produce super perfumes next to which the products of Dior, Chanel, Gucci, and so forth are manure) make up the veins that lead to these organs from all corners of the globe. These veins pump in nutrients, keeping the market supplied with the blood to sustain it.

The price some collectors are willing to pay for a single plant, a single living orchid, its species on the brink of extinction and strictly protected, often reaches perverse levels. It is absolutely nauseating. Decadent. While Kryštof was somewhat turned on by the degeneracy, it also viscerally disgusted him. He sometimes wondered how many rich buyers secretly rejoiced at the destruction of the rain forests, how many of them privately applauded the clearing of jungles and old-growth forests as it enhanced the prestige of their collections.

In his weaker moments, Kryštof was disgusted at himself most.

He always thought up a a little white lie to explain away his unease, to throw the blame on someone or something else, but deep down the guilt never stopped gnawing away at him.

He never completely admitted the raw truth to himself. The simple reality that it was he who was profiting off the speed of destruction. The speed at which humans were devastating Earth's biosphere. The speed at which we were effacing rainforests from the earth, as well as anything else seen as an obstacle to us for one reason or another, including an unfathomable number of plant and animal species. He didn't admit to himself that he was nothing other than an obscene salesman of disappearing life forms, flowers on their way out of existence. The sale of only four plants, perhaps the last of their species, was enough to keep him living comfortably for eleven months. Over the past few years, the pangs of conscience, swirling around him in an ever narrowing spiral, became harder and harder to dispel.

Kryštof got into this line of "work" completely by accident. While thinking about studying botany, he had started his own collection of flowers from what he'd stolen from Mr. Živný's greenhouse. After the old man's death, his son, Josef Živný (to Kryštof's surprise, he actually existed) intended to sell it all off for a pittance to the Prague Botanical Gardens. So when Kryštof was watering the old man's garden for the last time he secretly removed the most important specimens from the greenhouse.

He applied to university, and was rejected. He met Marián at the entrance exams, however, and this proved to be fateful. By chance they got into a discussion about the cultivation and breeding of tropical pitcher plants. That was Marián's great love — at that time he was exclusively focused on carnivorous plants. Kryštof had just become familiar with them, so Marián's extensive knowledge impressed him. They began to meet more often. Marián was accepted to university. He was soon letting Kryštof know about any important public lecture, and Kryštof, as much as his miscellaneous part-time jobs would allow, began attending them.

They spent an inordinate amount of time discussing the many areas of botany and the entire living world, driving each other's passion for the inconceivable richness of life forms on Earth's surface. They nourished in each other an awe for the intelligence and self-interest, at times malice and guile, displayed by all forms of adaptation, for the refined mechanisms of reproduction, for the genius of the biosphere, for the unknown when, how, and who had programmed the synergy of all life within the ecosystem. Where did evolution come from? This unbelievable progression from elemental, single-celled organisms to such super-complicated monsters as trees or humans? Why? Why did lowly cyanophytes and coreopsis not remain at the level of complete brilliance they had already achieved? Why does all life seek out some higher, more perfect form? And above all, how did anything animate ever develop from the inanimate? For what reason? Why did it take such a complicated path? At that moment death was also born! At that moment something arose that, over billions of years, would eventually develop into the sensation of pain! Not to mention that humans gained the ability to inquire into all of it, hopelessly and feebly, with no likelihood of ever attaining an acceptably precise answer. Kryštof often ended such reflections with one word. With one thought. That thought was God. Marián called it something else, but they were thinking more or less of the same thing.

In time, both of them came to grow orchids. It was a new perspective for them. An insight into true beauty. Kryštof often felt that orchids represented the attainment of perfection. That orchids were the point at which the evolution of all living forms had reached its pinnacle, a height from which it could only decline. A decline in which humans represented the most retrograde stage yet.

Neither of them had the money to set up a proper collection. Cultivating orchids without sufficient funds is practically impossible. Marián earned a little by growing pitcher plants. He sold them to various individuals for two to three hundred crowns a piece. Once he had earned six or seven thousand, he would buy an orchid he had coveted for several months. Kryštof always set aside something from his pay, but it usually took him half a year to accumulate the amount required.

And then Kryštof, with no real plan, came up with the idea that it would be better to go out and procure the flowers right where they were growing . . . in the rainforest.

They joked about it for a bit. But Marián unexpectedly took hold of Kryštof's idea. "Actually . . . why not?" he said, a bit unsure.

Over the following month Marián spoke about the trip more seriously. Kryštof was more cautious. He didn't believe they could pull off something like that. He had read several times about the harsh penalties facing anyone caught trying to transport protected plants without official permits (simply impossible to get for both of them). He knew that a number of countries had special police units targeting smugglers of endangered plants and animals. This sort of business frightened him.

During one of their meetings, Marián portentously declared it was time to plan their trip. He proudly and mysteriously told Kryštof he had found a buyer. He had made a contact willing to lend them the money for expenses on the condition they would bring back several plants for him. Overexcited, Marián tallied the regions where these rare breeds might reliably be found.

"So I would vote for Brazil. Manaus. It's a city in the middle of the jungle, I see that as a good starting point . . . Actually, I've already reserved the flight, so . . ." he said cautiously. Tense with expectation, he glanced at Kryštof.

Kryštof was silent. Adrenaline darkened his mind. He tried to imagine the rainforest. The place, he later discovered, was unimaginable. He still hoped that Marián wasn't serious, that it was only a premeditated joke.

Yet two months later both of them were sitting exhausted and pale with trepidation at the airport in Manaus, a backpack full of flowers at their feet. Devastated by the Brazilian jungle, they watched with bated breath the movements of the police through the airport. Unbelievably humid. The check-in line was getting longer. Nerves strained and painful from focusing so much attention on every movement around them. Their hearts pounded out the words that went through their heads, words occasionally said aloud in a vain attempt to allay the anxiety gripping them. Both of them felt as if they had committed murder or rape, and were just waiting for it to be discovered.

Kryštof couldn't handle it anymore. Standing up, he grabbed his backpack and headed for the restroom, a quick step alternating with a moderate trot. Marián frantically sped after him. He was breathing hard. This would certainly give them away. Several people looked over at them. Marián was sure they were screwed. He heard the pounding of police boots behind him. He quickened his step. He looked neither left nor right. On the back of his neck he felt the frozen spot where the barrel of a gun was pointing. Now the entire airport was certainly watching them. Marián squinted and prayed in his heart. He reached for the handle. Kryštof was vomiting in the sink.

He closed the door. He picked up the backpack flung onto the floor. He ran into the stall furthest from the entrance and locked it behind him. He unwrapped all the precious and beautiful plants they had spent the past month searching for and flushed them down the toilet. He watched the fragile flowers breaking against the water and porcelain. A month of two boys' lives disappeared somewhere into the bowels of airport plumbing. The last flower he flushed appeared on the extinct species list a year later.

When they got back into the airport hall nothing had changed. The usual commotion of travelers. The cold announcements of delayed flights in multiple languages, the scuffing of luggage in the check-in line. The calm conversation of dark-skinned police officers slowly making their rounds. Words, steps, yawns, a child's cry. Suddenly, extreme ease and emptiness. Fatigue. Adrenaline hangover. A numb feeling of peace.

In Prague they discovered that their journey had not been for nothing. Without even knowing it, they had imported six relatively valuable plants, which covered their travel expenses and left them with a little extra as well. It turned out Kryštof had bought three large souvenir conch shells painted with various silly decorations (Brazilian flags) in a shop the day before their departure and had threaded several plants into their coils. Although they silenced the roaring of the ocean inside the shells, customs officials fortunately did not discover them. He had packed the shells at the bottom of his backpack. Marián didn't know so didn't flush them. Kryštof forgot that Marián didn't know so was sure they'd been disposed of, too. Both of them were absolutely calm during check-in and everything went off without a hitch.

Without giving it a second thought, they set off to Bolivia nine months later.

•

They had known Nina since they were little boys. She often came to the cottage with her parents. At first they didn't take much notice of her because she was a girl, and her parents usually never let her go anywhere anyway. The disheveled and forever frowning Andrei and little, dirt-covered Kryštof spent most of the time in the forests or in the rubble of deserted Sudeten German homes. They crawled through half-crumbling cottages and barns overgrown with weeds. They were looking for something they could use as a weapon.

Andrei decided they would be hunters. As soon as they got their hands on a weapon, they would leave their parents and go live in one of the deserted military bunkers scattered along the border. They'd hunt deer and hares and not need anyone anymore. Kryštof once brought stale cigarettes he'd found in the pocket of his grandfather's old coat in the attic. They hid them in the bunker, and every time they went to the forest they would light one, pass it between them several times and puff on it, then extinguish it with spit, chew beech leaves, and wipe their fingers with them so that no one at home would know. Andrei said smoking kept away the wolves and boars, which Kryštof was afraid of. When Nina later joined them, she taught them to inhale (she was a year older than Andrei and always brought to the village some fine vices from the city). It made Kryštof ill. Andrei pretended he liked it and lit another one to prove it, but then threw up.

All three of them picked mushrooms, blueberries, blackberries, and many other things and stocked the bunker with supplies for winter. Andrei said seeds from pine cones were okay to eat, and so they collected those as well. They began building a second floor from spruce branches and ferns on the bunker's roof. They reinforced the walls with mud and laid a floor of grass and tufts of moss. Andrei and Kryštof set traps around the bunker. They would dig a hole in the ground about twenty centimeters deep and drive sharpened sticks into the earth at the bottom of it. Or they would bend over a young tree and pin down its top with a stone. They tied a loop to the tip, laid it out on the path, covered it with leaves, wound a fishing line around the stone, and stretched it taut between trees at ankle level.

Nina only played their games for a time. She got bored. Kryštof and Andrei were always going out to hunt, and she was supposed to guard their home until they brought back a kill. Andrei fastened the head of a pickaxe to a stick and carried a slingshot for firing bent nails. For Kryštof he fashioned a kind of pitchfork from branches and large screw hooks that had once reinforced bolted beams. Camouflaged in ferns, they lay still for long hours at the creek, waiting for an animal to come to drink. Andrei had infinite patience, Kryštof none. It often ended in an argument. They never caught anything.

Nina later began to think up her own games. They were all older by then, but Kryštof still didn't understand much of what was going on. Nina always gave Andrei a task. Maybe to steal something for her in the village. Then they met in the bunker. Nina took his hand and stuck it under her T-shirt. She held it firmly, stroking her body with it and sighing. Andrei never spoke with Kryštof afterward. He would get up and wander off. They'd already started growing apart.

Once Andrei went to the bunker alone and was about to go in when another guy came out of the dark and terrified him. Andrei turned and ran away screaming. The man was wearing a torn hunter's uniform, had tangled curly hair, the jaw bone of a deer hanging around his neck, and his face was smeared with mud. When he saw Andrei, he smiled, revealing black and broken teeth. They never went back to the bunker after that.

Kryštof fell hopelessly in love with Nina. He went to her once and asked her to give him a task, too. They met in the evening at a stack of hay bales in a field outside the village. They climbed inside one of the cavities. Nina let him stroke her wherever he wanted. She did not hold his hand like she did Andrei's. He believed it was a sign she liked him more. He closed his eyes and let his trembling hand read the Braille of her excited skin. Those touches intoxicated him. His breathing was fitful. His heart pounded against all the walls of his body. She then left him there alone. Before he opened his eyes again, an hour could have passed. He remembered nothing more from the rest of the day.

They met a few more times. There was never more than caressing and kissing. He was twelve. He had begun to discover the secret of moist breath and the aroma of another's body. He stopped speaking to Andrei. They didn't see each other for the rest of the summer. He was alone in the village with the taste of the girl's saliva under his tongue.

Once, when they were lying naked in the hay, Nina told him it was the last time. That she liked him very much, that he was a nice boy, but that she wanted to be with Andrei. She gave him a kiss and left. Everything in him turned bitter. He rose heavily to his feet, as if the whole world were flooded with water. His eyes burned. He walked past the fences and swallowed gall.

Andrei stole a rifle and started poaching. The first animal he bagged was a baby boar. He simply shot it. He stood above it. As if only they two remained on the entire planet, surrounded by the infinite autumn evening. The piglet breathed through the hole in its throat. It ate dirt in pain and spastically fluttered its hind legs. Andrei burst into tears, never having seen anything like it before. He shot it twice more before it was at peace.

Kryštof didn't come the next summer. He wasn't able to forgive Andrei for a long time. They nearly forgot about each other. They hadn't been in touch for years. Nine years later, Nina wrote Kryštof a letter. She wrote that Andrei had proposed to her. And they would like him to be their witness. Kryštof read the letter after the wedding was already over. He found it among the bills in his mailbox when he returned from Bolivia. He mailed a reply with an apology and a promise to visit soon, but he never went. Later, he found out about the birth of their daughter. They gave her the name Kristýna.

•

He stood in the cold night rain at the bus stop in front of the airport terminal. The light from the tall streetlamps accentuated every drop that fell from the sky. He watched the scratched glass of the telephone booth fragment the light from buses and taxis.

Marián, listen to me carefully, things have gotten a bit complicated . . .

. . . No, it would be better not to go anywhere right now, don't speak with anyone, don't answer the phone, don't call anyone. Someone is disrupting the plan . . .

Look, there must've been a leak. If I had flown through Vienna . . . I might be dead . . . The contact there . . .

Yeah. They found the body. I wouldn't want to see it . . .

Just be careful . . .

No, I don't know. When I'm in Prague, I'll come by . . . Or maybe I'd better not. They might be following me . . .

No, wait, don't do anything stupid, no one would be able to get there that fast . . .

Calm down. It might not be like that at all. I haven't slept for three days, maybe it's just starting to catch up with me . . .

Yeah. You, too.

He hung up.

Kryštof flew with a different airline from Tokyo back to Europe. He had missed the plane to Vienna. He needed to clear his head. He had drunk himself into oblivion in a nightclub and overslept the following morning. He bought a ticket on the next available flight to Prague with a stopover in Amsterdam. He was two days behind. In Amsterdam, he received a message that he shouldn't go to Vienna under any circumstances. Someone had eliminated the contact he was supposed to meet there. The body was found in a cheap hotel room on the outskirts of the city. Throat cut and mouth empty.

One day Kryštof decided to change his life. It suddenly occurred to him that after all those years he'd finally found what he was looking for. Or, rather, he rediscovered what he once knew. As time passed, he had pushed that realization as far away as possible. It was like a burning coal his whole being longed to grasp tightly in spite of the pain it would bring. A couple of her smiles would be enough to make up his mind. They didn't get a chance to speak together the whole evening. They touched with glances. Sometimes a gust of air would stroke his face when she walked past him. Nothing more. That was enough.

That's why Kryštof decided to accept the job. It was completely out of the ordinary. Marián was afraid of the assignment. He made all the arrangements, but otherwise refused to take part.

The job was to bring back a single plant from Japan. One tiny flower. A collector from St. Petersburg had commissioned it. He offered so much money that it blew both of them away. Kryštof took an advance and bought a house on the Polish coast with it.

Very little was known about the flower he was to steal. It was supposed to be a parasitic species. Extremely rare. Officially it was already long extinct.

He flew to Tokyo. Everything there went smoothly. This time he didn't have to trudge through any forests. The flower was growing right in town. In a small dilapidated garden house in the courtyard of an estate located in a dirty and remote quarter of the city. The trees were strung with lanterns. They rocked in the gentle breeze. The city center breathed and groaned behind him like some monster. He met no one but a couple of fifteen-year-old boys with black makeup under their eyes, long, dyed hair gelled to stick up, and dressed in tight leather pants. They were obviously on drugs and speaking a language that was all wrong. Japanese seemed to Kryštof like a cassette played backward. All the words were inhaled and swallowed.

It was two in the morning. He entered the dark courtyard. He looked around the dim space for a moment. He found his way to the small house in the moonlight. A wooden building, a broad roof with pieces of thatch missing like teeth, torn paper walls, rugs. The empty square shape of the floor. Outside crickets, otherwise silence. In the middle of the room sat a wide clay bowl covered by a lid with a massive handle. He took off his shoes and carefully stepped across the creaky floor.

He removed the heavy lid with both hands. He jerked. On the bottom of the bowl lay a cat. Dead.

No.

In the cold light seeping through the roof the cat's eyes suddenly shone. It raised its head feebly. It probably wanted to mew, but only emitted a kind of hoarse cackle. Its head wearily sank back down.

At first he thought there was nothing else in the bowl. He leaned inside and carefully stroked the cat. His trembling hand slid over its fur.

Then he felt something soft on its neck.

He flinched.

He knew what it was just by touch. It nauseated him a bit. He closed his eyes and took several deep breaths. The tiny coiled flower flawlessly blended into the night. It was black as coal. It grew directly from a wound.

He stood bent over the clay dish for a long time watching the withered feline body.

Finally, he decided.

He was walking through the strange city. All of Tokyo was suddenly silent. Out of the corner of his eye, huge lighted advertising panels mutely offered him all the world's wares. The shop windows across the street bent neon letters, car lights, and reflections of people. As he passed a nightclub, four hundred sweaty and drunk Japanese were hopping in front of a silent wall of speakers, but to the rhythm of his heart. He pulled his hood over his head. He was carrying his passport and a plastic box containing the rarest flower in the world in a plastic bag.

He'd had to uproot it somehow. He had to get it out . . .

It made a faint crackle.

Together with the cat's spine, he had broken sound. He had broken the sound of the world. From that time everything was silent.

•

From the diary of Antonín Brom, page 56.

September 1, 2002
The second person (a man whose identity long remained undetermined and whose connection with the K. Warjak case has only recently been established, but is now known to be Boris Styepanov) to whom Warjak

could deliver the flower was murdered with unusual brutality in front of witnesses in Prague on August 23, 2002, when he was returning home at night from Duplex Club on Wenceslas Square.

The murderer's identity is quite startling. Styepanov was killed by fourteen-year-old Pavel Blatný, who was blind! According to statements from two witnesses, this blind boy attacked Styepanov (who was quite drunk at the time) and killed him with his bare hands (he ripped out his carotid artery).

Blatný was found the next day in critical condition with a severe gunshot wound (shooter unknown) when an anonymous individual called him an ambulance. Blatný lay comatose in intensive care for two days. He died from kidney failure on the morning of the third day. Pavel Blatný's parents (Lenka Blatná and Petr Blatný) were devastated and horrified by the whole affair.

During questioning, they said their son had lost his sight four years ago from a serious concussion incurred in an automobile accident. Since that time he had sunk into a downward spiral of withdrawal. He was often silent, downcast, inaccessible. Pavel Blatný was a child of above average, more precisely, very high intelligence. For this reason, he never fit in with his peers, which only worsened with the loss of his sight. He had few friends, and those who sometimes visited him or took him outside befriended him mainly out of sympathy (as, according to them, Pavel Blatný noted several times). The entire situation came to a head a year and a half ago when he attempted suicide. He took an overdose of sleeping pills and subsequently underwent psychiatric treatment for severe depression. He ceased communicating almost entirely. He did not go to school. He shut himself off from the world. He was on a powerful antidepressant that caused him to fall into a state of complete apathy (if we were to take into consideration the possibility that Blatný was not in complete control of his mental faculties, we cannot rule out that he attacked Styepanov in a state of temporary insanity, a momentary loss of control).

Everyone around him had tried in vain to provide him with some distractions and socially re-engage him. His only expressed interest was the museum. It was his personal ritual. Daily visits to the National Museum. It understandably seemed strange to his parents that this could interest him when he could not see or touch the exhibits, but they did not dissuade him in any way. He once told them he felt at peace there. That reason was sufficient for them. At first, he went there with a chaperone, and later by himself. His trek to the National Museum was a daily necessity. His whole family was therefore tied to Prague by his needs, which no one ever regretted.

On Friday, August 23, 2002, Pavel Blatný again set out for his usual two-hour afternoon visit. That day he was unusually late. When he still did not return hours later, Lenka Blatná went to the museum to find out if her son was still there. Not finding him in the exhibition rooms, she inquired at the ticket counter when he had left the museum (due to his regular visits, P. Blatný was well known there), and was surprised to learn he had not shown up at all that day. Pavel Blatný did not return by eight p.m., at which time Petr Blatný contacted the police. A search was launched at ten that same evening.

•

Kryštof came in winter.

He filled those months with her image. With the shape of her lips, with the small wrinkle that formed by the left corner when she smiled, with her straw-colored hair, with her pale blue eyes. When alone, he would say her name aloud.

Nina.

It slipped through the air. Her prickly name ended inside his mouth. It emerged from a single bud on his tongue that still remembered the taste of her kiss from fifteen years before. Her name, thin as thread, strung together his every passing minute like the string of rowanberries she once wore around her neck as a child.

He brought her a flower he had cultivated long and diligently. He was painstaking in choosing the scent he wanted to remember her by later.

A thaw had set in. The snow was melting. The drain pipes clattered with water. He stood at the gate and waited. The sky was blue, interrupted only by electric power lines. The winter sun sparkled on the wet snow. It reflected off the water flowing down the street, off windows open wide to that whole new world to let fresh air pour into stuffy apartments again after such a long time. Kryštof's eyes began to well up from all the glint from windowpanes and snow crystals.

He squinted and listened to the sound of the day. Glass bottles shattered in a garbage can. Some boys around the corner were gleefully chucking one after another into the plastic dumpster. Somewhere behind a window left ajar was a kitchen. He heard a television, water, glasses, and plates clinking in the sink. The occasional rubbing of sponge and dish soap.

He rang a second time.

"Ok! Coming!" she called behind the window without even looking out. "I can't find my gloves!"

He'd been waiting fifteen minutes. They wanted to take a walk in the woods.

He had called her the day before and asked if he could stop by on the pretense that he'd be passing through. She was glad. Andrei was with Marián in St. Petersburg.

After many years, Kryštof returned one autumn to the village of his childhood. He wanted to see Andrei and Nina. He wanted to walk through all of those nostalgic places again. He also wanted to see little Kristýna. He was curious how she had blended the appearance and personalities of those two individuals into a new being. It was a beautiful two days. He arrived in the evening. Everything was wet. The smell of soil from the plowed fields. The lights were on in the cottages, and smoke from the chimneys rose up against the cold sky.

They sat at the table over their finished supper while Kryštof and Andrei remembered old times that didn't seem to belong to them any longer. Kristýna drew them a picture. Nina laughed a few times, but was otherwise quiet. Kryštof watched her out of the corner of his eye. She was gorgeous. Her face had retained a childlike gentleness. She really hadn't changed much over the years. She only looked a bit careworn. Tired. He observed her slender hands clear the dishes from the table. Her hands curl around a mug of tea. How she sipped, pressing her lips to the edge, as if giving the mug a peck. Then she said she was going to put the little one to bed. Everyone got a goodnight kiss. They listened to Kristýna sing while brushing her teeth so she wouldn't be afraid in the bathroom by herself.

When Andrei and Kryštof came back from the pub after midnight, Nina was already asleep. Andrei brought a bottle of slivovitz from the cellar, reached up to the shelf above the sink, slipped two fingers into and took down two shot glasses. They talked a long time, happy. Their talk flowed from one end of the table to the other. They filled in the abyss of years between their lives. Cold air brushed against them through the open window. It caught threads of their cigarette smoke and spun them outside into the darkness. Light from stars that might no longer even exist ended its journey of hundreds of millions of years on the wet leaves of the black elder. It cast a cool, silvery sheen over everything in the garden.

"But . . . why are you so interested in flowers?" Andrei asked when they came to the topic. He looked him straight in the eye, as if challenging him. "I just can't understand how you, of all people, picked something so . . . boring . . ."

Kryštof lowered his eyes and laughed. For a moment his finger traced a line back and forth in one of the wooden table's deep grooves. He crushed two salt crystals with a fingernail. Only then, a gentle smile still playing on his lips, did he meet Andrei's gaze.

"Well, parasites for instance . . ." Kryštof began slowly.

Andrei crinkled his eyebrows in confusion.

"Do you know anything about plant parasites?"

Andrei shrugged his shoulders and blew smoke through his nose.

"This was one of the first things that hooked me . . . Suddenly, I realized . . . these plants are truly alive. I don't know, you probably don't understand . . . Look. A stone is inanimate, it has always been like that, but a plant lives. The wood of this table is something that has died. It's a piece of something that once lived, and . . . Or like clothes . . . The real ones, not from synthetic materials. Flax fiber, that's something that once lived. Do you know what I mean?"

Andrei laughed. He wasn't getting it.

"Half of this house used to be alive," Kryštof continued. "Look," his gaze panned the room, "those floorboards, the beams in the ceiling, the stairs, doors, the tables, chairs . . . And all the cupboards, shelves, the bed you sleep in, all the books and all the pages inside them, the old newspapers by the stove, the window frames, the cooking spoons, the knife handles, everything! It all used to live inside a tree." He took a breath because it had all poured out too quickly. "Do you know what I mean? It grew together with that tree, convulsively stretching its leaves toward the sun, drank water with it from the soil and light from the sky . . . And all of this died with it . . ."

In the middle of the night they looked around at everything in the silent kitchen.

"You're living in a dead house." Kryštof laughed and licked his lips. "But what else . . . Look . . . What if plants feel pain and we ignore it? I know, I know . . . It's been roundly disproved . . . A shitload of scientific research . . . But what if all this has just been looked at in the wrong way? What if they find something in twenty years that overturns what they now think? Or what if it's all just a cover-up?" Andrei tried to say something, but Kryštof wouldn't let him get a word in. He raised a finger in irritation, cutting Andrei short, and went on, fascinated by his own voice. "Some species, like willows,when they get seriously injured, begin to send out such a strong chemical distress signal that it can do them more harm than the injury itself . . . so they start producing their own acetylsalicylic acid, aspirin, which they send through their sap to the injured area. They anesthetize themselves! What if they really do feel something and we're just not investigating it correctly? What if they have a kind of primitive consciousness?

"Plants communicate . . . they send out a variety of chemical signals that other plants and even loads of animals understand. Like tobacco, when it's attacked by caterpillars, it calls for help by releasing a substance into its environment that attracts ichneumonids, tiny wasps that kill the caterpillars by laying their eggs inside them! Or the acacia, which giraffes on the African savanna graze on. They're able to detect from the giraffes' saliva that something living is eating them and not the wind blowing on them, for example, and they then turn bitter so they won't be so tasty. At the same time, they send a warning to nearby bushes, which in turn become bitter when they receive the signal. And the giraffes then have to travel pretty far before they find any uniformed plants. It's absolutely incredible!"

Andrei did not try to interrupt Kryštof anymore. He listened and contemplated Kryštof's character.

"And it goes on . . . I mentioned parasites . . . They are such an amazing, bizarre group of plants! It's not a single family or order of plants . . . They occur in a variety of plant families, they are sort of renegades. Pariahs. In other words, cannibals . . . Holoparasites can't pass their genes on between host plants hereditarily. Each new individual parasite has to find its own new host . . . They've invented so many incredible mechanisms for this purpose. Like I said, plants communicate with each other through chemicals. Parasites are voyeurs. They eavesdrop on the chemical conversations of others! Like myco-heterotrophs . . ."

Kryštof tossed back a shot that Andrei (who was already beginning to get bored) had pushed into his hand. He breathed out, and before he even finished grimacing as the alcohol traveled feverishly through him resumed spewing words at Andrei.

". . . based on chemical signals they first sniff out potential hosts, a kind of green mycorrhizal plant, basically flowers whose root system is connected to a fungal symbiont . . . The myco-heterotroph sponges off the cooperation and mutual exchange between a green plant and a mushroom. It tricks the mushroom fiber by making roots that feign symbiosis. Then the confused mushroom feeds it, assuming it's the green plant it's connected to. Genius . . . ! Non-chlorophyllic subterranean parasites also have quite an interesting sex life. They don't waste energy with above-ground growth, obviously . . . They reproduce vegetatively in the earth and from time to time even reproduce sexually. A shoot usually doesn't have the strength to get above ground, so the plant flowers in the soil. Plants that bloom underground! White, sickly flowers. As if they were just milk skin. Fragile flowers that have sex with themselves, that self-fertilize."

Kryštof was speaking frantically. It wasn't clear if he was getting drunker on the alcohol or on his own talk. Andrei was barely listening anymore. He wandered with his thoughts around the room and then staggered with them to the front of the house. He went over what he'd have to do the next day . . .

". . . full parasites don't even resemble plants anymore. They aren't green, have no leaves, they behave strangely. Unplant-like. They present a problem for botanical taxonomy . . . They always pretend to be something else. They migrate from one family to another, from one order to another, as they are constantly reclassified . . . but the most amazing parasites are *Rafflesia*. *Rafflesia arnoldi* is a plant with the largest flower in the world. It grows in the tropical regions of Southeast Asia. Mainly in Malaysia and Indonesia. These plants prey on rainforest vines that create networks of wooden lianas. The only part of the *Rafflesia* above ground is its flower. Their roots penetrate the tissues and vascular clusters of the lianas and suck nutrients from their host. So it's nothing more than a flower . . . A flower with a diameter of one meter! A flower that weighs fifteen kilos!"

"Fifteen kilos? What?" Andrei's attention momentarily returned to the topic.

"Yeah. Incredible, right? *Rafflesia* is commonly called "corpse flower" or even "meat flower," because it smells like rotten meat. They live on the bed of a tropical rainforest, so they had to think up something to attract pollinators. And flies love the smell of rotten meat . . . Wherever the flower grows is considered a place of evil. The flower marks where the devil stepped when walking through this world!"

Kryštof paused. Andrei was looking somewhere out the window. When he realized the room had gone silent, he looked in Kryštof's direction, confused.

"I'm done . . . I got a bit carried away, sorry . . ." Kryštof laughed and ended the discussion in a calm voice. "I just wanted to say . . . What if . . . What if plants think on some level . . . ? How else would it be possible to explain all these incredible adaptive mechanisms? Plants are able to process a certain range of information . . . I would say that's a form of intelligence. Quite low, but still . . . Look, what's the difference between chopping down a tree, let's say a forty-year-old beech, and killing a cow or a horse or a whale? I don't think there's any at all. You're still killing something living and big. Both cows and trees think only about food and reproducing . . . No difference. Understand what I'm saying?"

Andrei nodded.

No one spoke.

Kryštof was deep in thought and said no more.

After a while, they stood up and, heads enflamed with alcohol, went out to the yard. They just stood by the fence a long time and listened to the quiet of the forest. Every so often they heard a faint rustling. Probably the owls combing the fields of mice. The cool October night extended into their nostrils. They were both tired. Back in the room, Andrei poured the last drops into the glasses. They clinked. Kryštof held his breath and swallowed. The liquor sliced into his stomach. He closed his eyes tightly.

He opened them the next morning.

They were walking on a forest path through wet snow. Nina, Kristýna, and Kryštof. They threw snowballs for a while, and Kristýna was soaked in no time. Kryštof lifted her onto his shoulders. They talked about silly things, whatever came to their minds. They made up alternative endings to fairy tales. They took turns at each sentence, but when it came to Kristýna, she always talked for at least five minutes. Nina smiled. Kryštof kept his eyes on her. She avoided them. He took her by the hand.

His memories kept bringing him back to his last visit. To the night he and Andrei had spoken again after so many years. He felt guilty. He also remembered the evening when Andrei first showed him the rifle. The night their lives had definitively parted ways. He clung to that memory. In an odd way, it gave him a contrived excuse for what he was doing here.

He kissed Nina on the cheek.

Kristýna was climbing up a deer stand.

Soft powdery snow shook off the rungs of the ladder. It emitted a sound the human ear is not capable of registering.

She lowered her eyes to the ground.

He moved his head away, but Nina caught his face gently in her cold palm and leaned it in to hers. She returned the kiss. This time on the lips. Her hot tongue slid into his mouth. So unbelievably hot in the surrounding world silenced by snow. The heat flowed through his whole body and remained somewhere in his head until the next morning when he left, filled with the scent of her fragile, childlike body.

Andrei had gone to Russia. He saved up a long time for the trip. He felt somehow attached to that country, he had to see it. It had been drawing him his whole life. He bought Russian grammar books and spoke fluently in a month. It was as if he had remembered something that had gotten lodged in the deepest recesses of his memory. He wanted to go to St. Petersburg to visit his grandmother, who sent a package of sweets to the orphanage every Christmas for his entire childhood. He'd never seen her and wasn't sure if she was really related to him. He hoped to find her by the return address on the packages. As Kryštof later found out, he didn't, she was no longer at that address. Andrei was told she'd been taken to the hospital three years earlier and had never returned. He spoke about his planned trip to Russia that autumn. It had surprised Kryštof. It was at the same exact time Marián was flying there to meet with a rich collector. Kryštof had been denied a visa. Andrei was going by train and had already bought the ticket. He wanted to see the countryside. In the end, Marián canceled his flight and joined Andrei. They became fast friends.

•

Krystof's life ended in the same place it had once begun.

He was watching the flickering of blood and light in his eyelids. I'll just rest a while. I'll sleep until morning, he told himself. I'll just get a little bit of sleep. He was breathing. He felt heat from the earth beneath him. In the black sky above him, a new constellation was forming. The bright Dog Star shone like snow. It bathed him in its light like his mother once had in a plastic tub when he still knew nothing but hunger. Everything was gently rocking, swinging, and carrying him away. He was floating over the surface of a meadow. If he put out his hand, it could slide over the waves of plant tips. He was falling asleep, and in a half-dream he reviewed his plans for the next day one last time.

Morning. I'll get up and walk down the train tracks to the closest village. I'll buy a ticket to Gdansk at the station and a pack of cigarettes from the beat-up vending machine. I'll walk around. The bench under the linden will have names and many other things carved into it. I'll slide my finger along the grooves and listen to the leaves above me with squinted eyes. The gravel will crunch when someone happens to walk by, or a dog will bark at the other end of the village.

The train will smell and rattle exactly as it should. People will be eating their snacks, lounging, occasionally someone will get up, leave the compartment and walk the aisle to stretch their legs. A guy will scratch his crotch on the sly. And children will ask if Mr. Conductor lives on the train or at the station. The landscape out the window will pass in the proper direction in relation to the direction the train is traveling, precisely according to plan. Children will leave their handprints on the glass and the floor will be covered with linoleum. Everything will be just right. Flawless.

From Gdansk he'll call Nina. She'll be feeling much better by then. She'll tell him that she'll join him. He'll hang up the smell of breath from each person who ever held the receiver. He'll hang up the electric, crackling breath of his beloved, the sound of her breath carried six hundred kilometers across cables and wires, underground and above it, through the air, the forest, over fields, assorted landscapes, through villages and towns, from house to house, through every intersection of branching electrical lines to here, to the telephone booth at the train station in Gdansk. Her breath transported here to him and him alone.

The house he bought for them to live in will be exactly as he had seen it the first time. A spacious overgrown garden with three old walnut trees. A few apple trees, plum and pear. The stone country cottage will serve as a reservoir of cold they will later scoop up in the watering can in the summer months and pour over the flower beds. It was an hour's walk from the village to a beach that was covered in snow in winter and rainy in summer, but when it was nice out you could walk along it for fifty kilometers in either direction without seeing another soul. They would be happy there. Precisely according to plan. This was Kryštof Warjak's final dream.

•

Noon
is dead quiet in the barley fields
nothing moving
for several hours, the same touch of kernels
the distances between stalks unchanging
perfect windless distances
the still touch of eyelashes
hours without blinking
the dry eye of a field
around a forest
bark peels from trees in the heat
wings rustle in the treetops
confused nocturnal birds
who couldn't fall asleep this morning

Heat bends the air over the road
on the asphalt glimmer patches of water
not there
Živný sits in the shade of a wayside shrine
amid a field
halfway to the village
breathing heavily
wiping his brow with a handkerchief
coming from a friend's funeral
thinking
how much time do I still have?
what sense is there in repeating every day
all these mundane things
sleep, eat, wash
each morning cutting off two millimeters of whisker with a razor
each would measure a kilometer if I let them be

each day shearing off that segment of tailor's tape
until military service ends
until civilian life begins
deaf and blind civilian life
deep in the dirt
That morning always in sight
the cemetery outside the village
bathed in sunlight
through the birch foliage
the blade of a buzzsaw heard in the distance
he stood at a hole
people had cut into the earth
for the dead to breathe

Everything coalescing since morning
with the stench of mothballs in his funeral suit
I don't have anyone anymore, he thinks
and wipes his temples and palms
sweat trickling under his shirt
I don't have anyone anymore

At that moment something thudded onto the ground
startling him
something had fallen into the nearby field
in the heat sounding like a louder heartbeat
like a dry gulp
from the spot the field sent out rings
like the surface of water disturbed by a stone

He stood
nothing happened

he went in that direction
ears of barley swished around his legs
rustling audibly in the surrounding silence
as black and white flecks swarmed before his eyes
seeming to him like a television's white noise

Silence
only crickets
rasping like plastic
he drank from the large hailstone
that had fallen into the field
he drank the strange water
emerging under the touch of his hand

He came down with fever that evening
and lay
his body merging with the dust of the universe
with water from another star cluster

The field where the hailstone fell
stopped yielding crops
and was covered with a toxic weed
that people call hogweed

•

Antonín Brom sat at the table peering at the pages of his diary he'd
left blank. He'd been taken off the case on account of his poor
health. The investigation was called off. He was nevertheless determined to report the events of that night. The night Warjak's body
was found and the subsequent autopsy. He was trying to understand

what had happened, but his attention constantly wandered, his concentration waned, his thoughts veered down dead ends. Too much was unclear.

The whole case seemed impossible to solve. The murders of Khalkin and Styepanov were not committed by the same person. Baumgarten and Blatný had no contact with anyone in Russia, Japan, or with each other. Although everything was still being corroborated, it was already evident that no one had paid them. The possibility of their being hired killers could virtually be ruled out. They had even begun investigating whether Baumgarten, or even Blatný, had been under the influence of someone or something.

A psychologist, an expert on hypnosis, had been brought in on account of Baumgarten's amnesia, which was definitively confirmed after a thorough examination. Unfortunately, this delivered no conclusive results. While Baumgartner did exhibit some post-hypnotic symptoms, such as disorientation, confused and sporadic behavior, immoderate reactions to certain stimuli and so on, when a hypnotic state was induced and the hypnotist tried to cancel any potential post-hypnotic suggestion and recover memories of the time when he killed Khalkin and came to Prague and attacked Rotko, Baumgarten said nothing. It seemed his memory was truly blank here . . . He willingly answered all the other questions he was asked under hypnosis. Yet Baumgarten didn't, or couldn't, recall anything from August 19 to 22.

They were also unable to discover anything about to whom Warjak was supposed to deliver the flower. That the person was from Russia could be assumed only from the nationalities of all three contacts. Bardyaev, the only one they found still alive, couldn't be interrogated because he had to be hospitalized. It was also incomprehensible why someone so indisposed had been selected as the key intermediary, the connection, the one to take charge of such a priceless item. Bardyaev, with late-stage lung cancer, hardly able to breath, every movement requiring an enormous effort from him . . . how could it be that someone like that had been chosen?

Far too many variables were not known. But after what Brom had experienced during Warjak's autopsy, he was no longer seeking any resolution. After all, the investigation was no longer his concern. Except for the fact that he'd been questioned about gaps in the case file. Detective Josef Kabala, who took over the case, had complained that some of the reports were incomplete. Rightly so. Brom had consciously withheld several facts. He'd mentioned nothing concerning one aspect. The flower.

Brom fixed his eyes at a point in the center of a blank page. Everything converged at that bizarre point, at the event that had caused his current condition. He could not find enough peace of mind and the distance necessary to write that passage. He was now incapable of talking about it with anyone. He couldn't even talk with himself about it. From the time Podlipský told him the type of plant it was, he was fairly sure he wouldn't survive. What had happened to him. What he had in his left arm. He was absolutely unable to write anything about the event in his diary. He'd left those two pages blank. Amid the pages of dense writing those two blank sheets, when he looked at them, seemed to say more than any words he could possibly put down.

He reread the last entry.

August 26, 2002

Discovery of the flower.

Last night I was present at Warjak's autopsy. The pathologist cut open the stitches poorly sewn to close the wound in Warjak's side. The assistant fastened clips to the edge of the wound to open it and suddenly looked at us in shock and surprise. He froze. He was not able to complete his movement. The pathologist, who had just been speaking with me, stepped closer to the table to see why his assistant was so startled. He immediately stopped talking . . .

Inside the wound was a flower. The small, black, coiled blossom of an unknown plant. We exchanged baffled glances for a moment. I thought it over. I finally nodded to the pathologist to remove the flower.

We discovered that something was holding it inside the wound. He managed to lean the flower to one side and revealed that its roots (emerging directly from the flower itself) had grown into the body. We were amazed to find they were the very same fibers that had been tangled throughout the area where Warjak's body was discovered. I was unsure of how to proceed. None of us were ready for this. None of us had ever seen anything like this.

Before I was able to say anything or react in any way, the pathologist cut several roots with his scalpel. He was about to remove the flower, and I immediately thought to stop him. This phenomenon should be studied in situ, undisturbed. All of us abruptly jumped away from the table in fear.

The entry stopped there. Brom couldn't go on. He didn't know how to describe the following events, though he remembered every detail. The milky lamplight above the autopsy table. Everything cold. The sharp sounds of the surgical instruments on the side table. The handles of the hospital cart. Three pairs of eyes moving above surgical masks full of the sterile smell of disinfectant. The chill coming from the dead body. Professional movements in a silent room. The white and green hospital smocks. The white, bloodless pallor of the dead skin, through which branching violet veins shone in places, reminiscent of the underside of a leaf or an aerial photograph of a large river. The violet wound on the belly opened with clips. The flower.

The stroke of the scalpel. Brom shot out his hand to stop any further movements. Chills went up his back. As the startled pathologist jerked back his hand he unintentionally cut Brom across the wrist. It stung. like being cut by grass. A blade of sawgrass. Small drops of blood ran from the incision, reminding him of mercury.

The flower moved.

It gave a faint pop. It uncoiled. It opened as quickly as an eye. At the precise moment the pathologist cut through the roots to remove the plant from the wound. The flower was black. Without any line or pattern. Only a dense concentrated black. The plant began slowly, as if groggy, withdrawing its remaining roots from the dead body, reeling them in with a soft, wet hiss, a quiet muffle that sounded through the entire corpse.

He watched that slow movement in disbelief, weighing what to do. Should he stop it? Run to get someone else? He didn't know. He decided to wait.

The instant the plant had completely withdrawn the ends of its first two shortest roots from the body, something unexpectedly quick occurred. Brom scarcely perceived it at all. The plant swung both the free roots in his direction and slipped their ends right into the fresh cut on his wrist. It was as if two hypodermic needles had pierced him. Only much deeper. He felt the sensation run from his wrist through his forearm, his biceps, and to his shoulder.

He screamed.

The assistant knocked over the instrument table.

Metal clattering to the floor.

He couldn't imagine what might have happened if the pathologist had not kept his composure and immediately cut both tendrils.

He then turned to the autopsy table and cut all other roots, killing the flower.

This was the story of that night. Never before had he experienced something so terrifying. Four years to go to retirement. If someone brought in all the official reports he had written in his career, there would be no space left to move. Now, despite all his practice and experience in submitting precise descriptions of the bodies of murder victims, administrative reports, and statements full of the horrors he had long ago stopped seeing as out of the ordinary, he'd been sitting three hours over two blank pages of his diary, intentionally set aside for this entry, and he was incapable of writing a single word.

He rose heavily from the table and paced the room. The wooden floor creaked beneath the carpet. He paused at the window and observed the people in the apartments in the opposite building for a moment. He watched various silent actions in lit rooms. Evening was falling. September was tainting the leaves. Entire crowns of trees were dying. A bit longer and the trees would reach the zero position. Everything living would retreat beneath the surface. Into the roots. Into their mirrored reflection of branches beneath the soil. The world of trees turned upside down.

He turned on the light, and an old lady at a window in the building opposite, also secretly watching the evening stories of strangers, turned her head in his direction.

They called off his whole team. Everyone who had been in Těchonín that night had been stricken with an odd sort of asthma and unusual liver problems. He would most likely lose his arm. He'd lost all feeling in it. He couldn't move it, and it was completely cold to the touch. A dead part of his body. As if it didn't even belong to him anymore. The doctors were at a loss. No toxins were discovered in the limb, nor were any other pathogens. Blood was not flowing into it. His whole circulatory system was simply avoiding it as if it were something alien. As if it had gone to sleep. Forever.

ANDREI

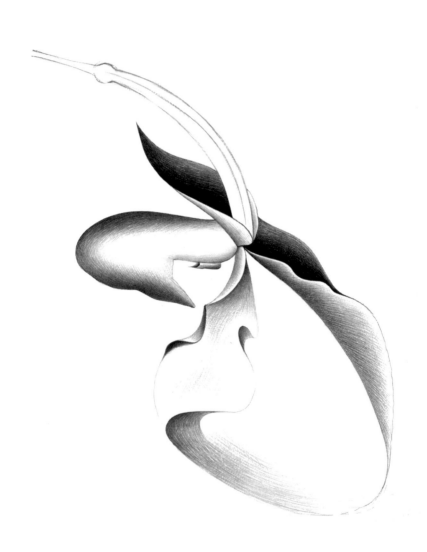

Deer tracks.

A spoor.

The evening sky clear, particles of frost poured from black trees. One never walks alone in the snow. Over the years Andrei had come to know these woods better than anyone. He set out in the afternoon while it was still light. He walked fast, thrusting his feet forward into the fresh layers of snow. He had to stop every so often to brush off his pant legs and dig out the hard chunks of ice from behind the tongue of his boots. He didn't want to get too wet. It usually got dark around four o'clock and so freezing at night that breathing was a chore.

He walked down old overgrown forest paths. He could follow them clear to the Polish border. But Andrei left the path around three kilometers from the village and made his way deeper into the forest among the dead blackberry brambles and low trees bent under the snow. Dusk fell. The whole world went silent. Only the faint flickering of a comet's tail could be heard from somewhere out in space.

Andrei paused and strained his ears until they whistled inside. The silence was so intense here it was often audible. He pressed on. The snow again eddied around his knees as he plodded his way forward.

He'd changed over the past few years. After completing forestry school he began working as a logger. He cut down trees. He cut off their branches with a metal chain and exposed the light beneath their bark. Bare trees shone yellow. A fragrant light seeped out in golden drops, and when Andrei placed his hand on a sticky stripped trunk, he felt it subtly warming him, as if something were still alive within it. In time, Andrei learned to exist in a way strangely connected to other things. As if everything was flowing around him, some things slipped through his mind the same way he breathed or touched what surrounded him, but nothing lingered inside him. He felt no imperative, nothing indispensable.

He pulled off the scarf wrapped across his mouth and nose. It was already soaked from his breath. He pulled a tin flask out of his breast pocket and drank. The warmth of the liquor flowed through his body. He took one more swig, rewrapped the moist scarf around his face, and tied a bow under his chin to secure the earflaps of his cap. He might have to spend the whole night in the frost. Somewhere out on the airless, endless mountain slopes, in places where, for fifty years now, the landscape had been gnawing away at the remains of deserted villages.

He would occasionally pass through eerie places, pause, and allow that space to circle his body a few times, then turn twice around to get a proper look at it all. Among the tall beeches, oaks, and firs would suddenly be flat ground where only a handful of fruit trees grew. A building must have stood here, the outlines of individual rooms still lying sprawled beneath the snow. In summer he'd come across a similar spot where he could make out the foundations of a house just faintly emerging from the forest dirt. He saw where the kitchen might have been, the living room, a cowshed.

As a small boy he often climbed through deserted dwellings,

observing how quickly weeds overtook them. He enjoyed returning to those places where trees grew right up through the middle of empty houses, tearing through the roof to get out, houses where roof beams were so worm-eaten they crumbled to dust in your hand, houses where black elder thrived.

Once he saw a doe grazing in a small ruined chapel, but she didn't run away as he approached. She froze and looked at him. He inched forward and stretched out his hand to touch her . . . and suddenly he was struck by the eeriness of the encounter. It almost made him afraid. How could she be so unnaturally tame? He turned and briskly walked away, keeping her in view over his shoulder. When he got far enough away, she began grazing peacefully again on the grass covering scattered graves.

When he told Nina about it later, she remembered a dream she'd had as a little girl. In the dream, she and other children mistakenly wandered into a forbidden place in the forest where they met a rare, nearly extinct white deer, unique because it subsisted on meat, a carnivore. "Then we just ran. I was the last and I woke up the moment I felt it bite the hair on the back of my neck." This is what Nina told him.

He reached the place where he'd set his traps two days before. It was now getting dark, though visibility was still good. The moon and stars illuminated the forest with a cold clean glow like the glint of metal. He checked the steel wires. They were all empty and untouched. Andrei needed meat. A doe, a faun, anything. Nina still had no work and little Kristýna was in bed with a high fever. They had a measly eight hundred crowns until the next payday, and they needed money to get the car fixed.

He came across the concrete bunker buried in snow. It was nearly impossible to make out from its surroundings as snow covered it up to the roof, but Andrei was sure this was the place. Their bunker. The one from their childhood. He trudged toward it through the heavy snow. He usually avoided the place. But now the situation was different. Everyone avoided this area. Hunters especially. But he needed a doe, or at least a hare. His spirit was lifted by how quickly he'd made it here, it was an orientation point, about half a kilometer to the border.

He stopped at a tree trunk and carefully observed the knoll beneath the snowdrift. He'd already seen tracks. A dull milky light shone through the snow amassed against the bunker's window. As if it were shining somewhere deep underwater, on the bottom of a river or lake.

He warily skirted the bunker and stepped further into the forest as quietly as he could. Folks told lots of stories. He'd heard them as a boy. About a deranged hunter who spent too much time in the forest. He fled from the whole world to the woods. He shot animals nobody else could see. They materialized in his painfully crooked mind. He was said to have been a bus driver who fell asleep at the wheel once and crashed. Two people lost their lives. He did time because they'd detected traces of alcohol in his blood from the night before. He never got over it. In the end, he lost himself in the forest. Folks said his shots couldn't be heard and that later he started hunting with his bare hands. They said he once killed a deer with his bare teeth. He silently walked the wet animal trails, and no one walking in the forest could ever be sure he wasn't standing right behind them.

Andrei checked the traps set in other areas. He was now chilled to the bone. He felt the cold gnawing away at his life. The areas of heat in his body were shrinking. His hands and feet were numb, bloodless. He tried to think about that warm place within him.

About the last warm place in the December forest. He returned home. Every eye was hollow. The third day of nothing.

•

The evening Kristýna died, something was torn from Andrei forever. Something human. The whole day repeated itself in his head, tossing and turning like a dog in mud. The endless carousel of minutes and hours, seeking something to help him overcome the pain. He knew very well that nothing like that existed, it was pure despair, a void where he kept encountering himself alone.

From that moment, Andrei couldn't see the point in anything anymore. His life had suddenly and definitively lost all meaning.

It's like a crack in the ice, he told himself
a channel of air for lake water
at the beginning of spring
a pale blue channel
raw as neon
against the morning sky
I run my finger along it
from that moment
ever further from shore
further into silence

He got up before seven a.m. Nina was asleep, but the moment the tips of his toes touched the floorboards and the wood creaked faintly, he knew she'd open her eyes. He didn't turn to her, he reached for a cold shirt and threw it over his shoulders.

She observed him buttoning his shirt and pulling on pants still damp with dew from the night before when he'd come back from the pub. She observed the quick jerk with which he tightened his shoe laces, and as he pulled a woolen sweater over his head, she noticed the left sleeve was torn. I'll have to mend it, she thought.

When he turned toward the door and was about to leave the room, she propped herself up in bed on her elbows.

"Wait," she said and was startled by how hoarse her voice was from the cold night. Andrei released the door handle and looked back at her.

"I need to tell you something."

He frowned and sighed. He was supposed to be at work at seven-thirty.

"Come on, just for a moment." She paused and then added, "it's important."

Andrei went back to the bed and sat beside her.

Half an hour later little Kristýna was awoken by the loud bang produced when Andrei slammed the door on his way out. He crossed the yard at a furious pace.

Nina sat on the bed looking at the wall. She held her busted lower lip in her teeth and sucked blood from it. She sat like that for nearly an hour. Kristýna came to her and curled up in her lap, a small animal full of warmth.

That morning, Nina admitted to Andrei that she had cheated on him with Kryštof. While he was with Marián in St. Petersburg. Kryštof had come once to visit them. He said he loved her. That he'd always loved her. She made a mistake and was admitting it. Now it hurt her, a lot, and she was so sorry she'd done it. She couldn't get it out of her mind.

"You were completely closed most of the time, hardened, you know, I don't even know when you kissed me last, Andrei, or caressed me or even just looked at me sweetly." She peered at him, imploringly, horribly unhappy. She tried to catch his gaze. That angered him all the more.

"I was completely wilted, empty! Look, I need to know you feel something for me, that this life isn't just leading into emptiness." Tears rolled down her face.

"It's easy for you to just pack up and go off into the forest for two days, but what about us? What about Kristýna? She's always asking me, where's daddy? When is daddy coming home? Can we go to see him? And you? You come home and pay no attention to her, you eat and sleep . . . even if you feel nothing for me anymore, at least you could for her . . ." She wiped her face with her hand. Eyes lowered, he clenched his teeth and flexed his jaw.

"And if you're not in the forest, you're out drinking, you've been hitting it really hard these last two years, you know we have no money to spare, and still you drink through more than all three of us eat. That's how it is! So say something!" She was almost screaming at this point.

"Dammit, you didn't even remember Kristýna's birthday, you were off again who knows where. I walked into town and back that day to buy her at least something, a book of fairly tales, you came back at night hammered, after she'd gone to bed. I let you sleep on the kitchen floor under the table where you flopped down. Do you remember that? Do you understand what I'm saying? This is no way to live, I can't do it anymore! Say something! At least one goddamn word! Do you remember getting into a fight? How you came back with your mouth busted, eyebrow torn up, completely covered in blood and full of vodka? She was afraid of you! Your own daughter! Do you hear me? *You* betrayed us!" Her voice cracked.

Andrei straightened up and hit her in the face as hard as he could.

She shrieked.

"You betrayed me," he said in a quiet, trembling voice.

He turned and left. Confused, full of bitterness and rage. Everything around him started to swim. He walked to the village square and beat on the pub's window. He bought a bottle. Before he got to the sawmill, where everyone met to leave to the job site, he'd finished half of it. He got an earful about being late. In the deafening metallic clamor of the truck, he watched the muddied forest road. He breathed in the reek of gasoline, oil, and cigarettes. They periodically passed piles of cut logs along the way. They were his calendar. He could precisely count back the past days from the progression of clearing as the cutting gradually moved deeper and deeper into the forest. He reviewed each day of the previous month of his miserable life. It was drizzling.

All day underwater. Earplugs muffling the roar of the chainsaw. The absolutely silent movements of figures killing a forest. The aroma of tree viscera. Sawdust raining over the grass and moss. Soundless talk and laughter. Nina. Her body. His gloves black from oil. Another tree sailed through the air like a silent shot of an oar. The throbbing motor in his hands. The heart of the machine. Sliced growth rings full of sap. The sharp pain of hunger in his stomach amplified by the raw alcohol. The taste of metal in his mouth. Gums. Bitter tobacco saliva and hot breath.

They came back around five. He walked slowly, light shining in windows. The sky was draped in a dense, dark film of gray. The fine rain incessantly falling on roofs and fences grew into a downpour. A sheen like a dim mirror was cast over the street. Broken, black asphalt. Water roared from a cracked sewer cover. He didn't know where to go. His head was spinning and he felt an abysmal fatigue. He was drunk, but not enough to relax him. He wasn't thinking about anything anymore, senses thoroughly dulled, water ran from his hair across his face and lips, sometimes trickling in tiny streams to his collar and under his shirt. He took shelter beneath the roof of a house. He stood and numbly observed the threads of water being spun out of the overflowing drainpipe.

A window opened beside him. The metal hooks securing the shutter against the wind rattled against the windowsill.

"There was an ambulance at your place," said an old man, whose name Andrei no longer remembered.

"What?" Andrei moved closer to the window, hunched under the torrent of rain, his arms clutching his chilled body. "When? Why?"

"I don't know, probably two hours ago."

Andrei just nodded and ran into the deafening downpour.

The door wasn't locked. He turned on the light in the hall and went into the kitchen. The house was quiet. They were gone. The telephone receiver hung on its hook. He lifted it and held the regularly punctuated sound to his ear. He hung up.

The number for the hospital . . .

He couldn't remember.

He picked up the receiver again. One, five, five.

"Yes, we are connecting you."

. . .

"Unfortunately, there's no one by that name . . ."

"How's that? They came here . . ."

"No, wait, one moment, here it is, yes. One more moment . . . I'm connecting you with the attending physician . . ."

Nothing but the hollow sounds of a hand covering the other end of the receiver. The rustling of sleeve fabric, the creaking of an office chair's wheels, and the slap of the phone cord against the edge of a table. A deep, tired voice.

"Good evening . . . I have some bad news for you . . . I'm very sorry to inform you . . ." Coughing . . . "Your daughter has died of poisoning resulting from the ingestion of mushrooms . . . Your wife has also been poisoned, and for the moment we cannot say if she will make it." A short pause, a breath. "Please, don't do anything rash, come to the hospital if you can. This was a suicide attempt . . . in your wife's case, that is, the mushrooms were all highly toxic, she collected them herself, as she told us, she also called the ambulance afterward, your daughter actually . . . by accident, ate the rest of the food your wife prepared from the mushrooms, and unfortunately, it was a fatal dose for her system. Please try not to do anything rash. We will need to speak with you. The police will, too . . . Can you hear me? Hello? Are you still there . . . ?"

Andrei hung up.

•

Torn off leaves in brown currents
showed their light bellies
he stood on the bridge outside the village
the downpour over
the last light of evening suspended over the forest

Giants drops fell through the air
from the clean drenched trees
it is already so long ago
in a distant garden someone was chopping wood
he gazed into the water
its speed made his head spin
the village was quiet
only the sound of logs coming unstuck

regularly measured out the moment

He ran with all of his power
away from there
away from the riverbank
he ran and everything in him ripped apart
he tripped over plowed up roots
blind white vines full of water
rapidly dying in our world
accustomed to breathing through soil
he grabbed onto them
as he clambered up the track made in the slope
when horses had dragged the wood to the paths
he tore those veins out of the great body
his feet slipped from under him on the wet earth
he cried out in rage and kicked the dirt
he pounded his fists into it, tearing off a piece of skin
and again launched himself upward
he fell again and then only lay there
and with him all the trees cried from their viscous wounds

He breathed
he smelled the sap of spruce
bitter tree honey
a flock of sheep emerged from the woods
quietly grouping in the evaporated water
the sound of barking in the distant village
the darkness of that night began in the nostrils of dogs
oozed out of them and into the landscape
and soon flooded over him
somewhere on the western slopes

he heaped up dirt for entire hours
covering himself in it
he stuffed it into his mouth and eyes
he became one great mycelium
a couple weeks later, in that spot, grew mushrooms
no one from the village recognized
and everyone avoided eating

•

From that time Andrei was someone else. He awoke weeks later in an unfamiliar place. He had a vague recollection of walking through the forest raving. He had raked his body over stones. He had carved into his arm with sharp pine bark. He had drunk sap straight from trees and eaten rotting leaves. He wanted to poison his blood. He wanted to die as part of the forest, merge with it. He wanted to dissolve into the soil. He wanted to transform into something else, become a plant, something of a lower order that still didn't know how to feel pain. And so he lost himself. He fell asleep somewhere deep underground.

The place he woke up in was cold. At first he thought he was inside a cave, but when he reached for the wall he found it was perfectly flat, made of concrete. He was lying on dry spruce branches. They poked and scratched his body. On his face he felt something dried up, peeling. The atmosphere around him was suffused with acrid smoke and a strangely sweetish aroma.

He tried to stand, but found he was unable. He was too weak. As he slowly looked around, he noticed a bottle beside him. He reached for it. It was an ordinary crumpled plastic bottle full of water. It tasted like mud. He felt a sort of package near it. Something wrapped in fabric. He unwrapped it. It was a hard hunk of bread.

He ate and drank the little he could manage to get inside him.

He lay back heavily onto the needles and thought. The dream that woke him seemed impossibly long, lasting perhaps weeks, months, whole years, even. All his previous memories suddenly felt extremely distant. He didn't know which reality was more substantial. Whether everything he'd previously experienced or what had happened in his sleep. Yet he was sure both of them were equally real. The pain he felt in both was the same.

The dream had begun with a long fall, an endless feeling of vertigo. Like when a swing stops in one spot for a fraction of a second and the pressure in the body deliriously rises up through the throat into the head, but this moment was prolonged for many hours. It intensified to the brink of insanity. Inside his body, bliss mixed with an unbearable tension.

It lasted an eternity. He flew through darkness. He met no resistance, no air whistled past his ears, his hair didn't flutter in the wind. It was just falling. A pure and perfect falling. He could think of nothing but the endless pressure inside him. Everything accelerated with the beating of his heart, pounding in his throat. He fell for so long that he slowly forgot any other motion he'd ever known.

A change finally came.

He hit a surface. The impact was horrific, but absolutely silent. He could hear only the sounds of his body. He felt his spine shatter. Several of his ribs poked out through his belly, strange bony talons with overly long nails. His entire right arm cracked wetly as it twisted out of his shoulder joint and lodged itself inside his rib cage. This caused his lungs to burst, and he started suffocating. The impact crumpled him and molded him back into the form of a grisly embryo. Yet he was unable to die. Oddly, though he felt all the pain so precisely and acutely, he knew it would not free him.

It was also odd that he'd hit the surface from the opposite side, because when his body had shattered it (as it shattered him), he shot up out of it enveloped in a column of water, like a geyser, high into the air above an expansive lake. Before the water pulled him back in, he observed the lake's surroundings. Several birds startled by the sudden geyser shooting into the sky flew from the tops of trees along the shore. He even thought he saw a person, maybe a fisherman, but he couldn't be sure. The sun was shining.

He reached the apex of his ascent and started to fall back. Rays of sun sparkled in the spray of water amidst a beautiful summer's day. He summoned all his strength to free his disfigured body from the column of water. He felt it was his last chance to save himself. He thought he could wrest a mouthful of air outside of it. But the water held him tight, as if with two great arms and about to swallow him. He gave up trying to free himself. He firmly shut his eyes and locked himself into the pulsating scream of his devastated body. He slipped back into darkness.

Hands tossed him to a floor of tamped earth. His eyes bulged in a scream as a cold metal rod grated its way through his shin bone. The hollow ringing of iron as someone pounded it with a hammer. They were nailing him to the floor. The other leg followed, then his left arm and right shoulder (that is, the place his shoulder had been). He became delirious, unable to endure more.

The room or space he found himself in started to swing and heave in time with the blood pulsating in all his wounds. Dark figures moved around him. They led in a girl, a small child, she was naked and had seven mouths. One on her throat, another on her belly, on her thigh, on the nape of her neck, one in place of her left eye, one in place of her genitalia, and one where it would normally be. She started eating the flesh off him. He was unable to faint, all he felt now was terror. Mortal terror and revulsion. Someone removed his kidneys and liver, tore out his heart, and coiled his veins into a big ball. They opened his head at one of his cranial sutures. They extracted his brain and withdrew the spinal cord from his vertebrae. They finally pulled out his eyes, slightly altering his visual perspective. His remaining organs and blood were eaten by the girl with her seven maws.

Only his bones remained. A hammer pulverized them. All this was gathered up and thrown into a cauldron, under which a fire was being kindled. His perception of this phase was hazy, out of focus, but he was aware they were adding strange ingredients to the cauldron. Crow's eyes and herb-paris, mercury, cow's stomach, swan necks, alcohol, tobacco, and other similar items. They brewed it for months. No one tasted it, just stirred it occasionally.

The flow of time had been completely altered. Pain turned to numbness, to deafness. The cauldron's brew whirled like the night sky. The cold light of stars shone in it. As if the cauldron were boiling down a piece of the universe. The water took on the form of unknown galaxies, the most remote undiscovered constellations. Strangely, it wasn't boiling, it was almost chilled, though they continually fed the flames beneath it. Finally, after an unfathomably long time, oblivion came, a liberating peace. Peace, silence, and cold, like after a supernova burns out.

After the endless procession of solstices and seasons that must have passed, they took the cauldron off the flames and fished out numerous shards and bone fragments. It was like waking up in broad daylight. They tossed them onto the floor, and all those shades — those strange dark figures — sat around them and commenced piecing each individual fragment and splinter back together. It was long, niggly work. There were thousands and thousands of shards, and they kept pulling more from the cauldron.

Every time two bone pieces were found that fit together, they fused on their own. The integration of every single microscopic particle was essential. He gradually felt his thigh bone cohere, his ribs and lower jaw form, the millimeter by millimeter growth of his vertebrae joining his spine like a snake, and, after a half-year of work, he felt the wonder of being able to crack the bare knuckles of fingers on a newly created hand.

This procedure also took a great deal of time, though now it passed differently. It was an enjoyable activity, and constructive in the true sense of the word. What's more, it was absolutely painless. The bones cohering pleasantly tickled and slightly itched as life returned to them. Everything was new. Full of expectation. His original fear of what would follow after the parts of his body had finished cooking faded and transformed into curiosity.

With his skeletal system finally whole, they began to set his organs into it. The heart first. No sooner had they pulled it from the cauldron than tendons and muscle fibers sprouted from it. Veins coiled around it, whipping around and twisting. In no time his heart hung inside the rib cage, fastened to it by strips of meat like some bizarre beast and emitting strange sounds not unlike the whimper of a child breastfeeding. Blood vessels began to uncoil, ramifying like ivy and slowly creeping over the bones, cautiously inspecting the path before them by casting smaller vessels as feelers.

Flesh grew everywhere veins crept along the bones. The body was progressively dressed in musculature that was then covered in connective tissue and all consolidated with tendons. The blood vessels wove themselves throughout this proliferation, stabbing their tiniest and sharpest veins into the freshly produced flesh and setting down roots in it.

Meanwhile, they had placed the liver, kidneys, and brain into his body. In the same way, these organs were alive and moved the instant they emerged from the cauldron. Once in the body, they were immediately punctured by thousands of minute capillaries, and large fat arteries fastened onto them like blue leeches. The remaining organs grew spontaneously on their own. Skin began to cover his body. Before it became completely encased, they placed a small pinkish stone just under his lungs, and veins latched onto that as well.

Lastly, they set his eyes into his head. Their color had paled to gray. They were most likely not the same ones they'd taken from him. He blinked a few times. And then his heart beat for the first time. It hurt a bit. Warmth surged through his body to its furthest extremities. He had completely forgotten how it felt. He'd lived whole years in cold. He moved his hand. The first sacred touch of his own body. He ran it over his face and rubbed his eyes. He stretched. An incredible bliss flooded him from head to foot. He stood and took several careful steps.

He discovered that a thick living cord led into his belly. He bounced off the floor and floated through the air and to the ceiling by waving his arms a few times. He turned over twice and glided freely. He kicked at the wall because the space had shrunk. Everything around him throbbed and rumbled in regular intervals.

He was alone. Several acute and persistent thoughts arose in his mind that he didn't at all understand . . . He had been initiated. He had received a new mind and body. An important meeting awaited him. He must be prepared for it. A certain principle had seeped into his nervous system. A certain mental code spreading like a virus through the human world. People called this code a curse or hex. For a short time he would be under the complete control of this principle. The stone placed inside his body would soon start to behave like a disease. It was a fail-safe. The only way to rid himself of the stone was to fulfill the curse . . .

Everything lurched. A massive contraction of the entire space was pulling him somewhere outside. He tried to grab hold of the slippery walls. The walls were alive. He didn't want to leave this place. He feared what was outside. Within moments the pressure stuffed him into a narrow opening, through which a larger body painfully expelled him with several more contractions. He breathed and started to scream in the intense light of day.

•

Andrei finally got to his feet and, staggering, hand against the wall for support, slowly walked through a narrow corridor. A single exit led from the tiny space where he'd woken up. Light illuminated the corridor through narrow openings. They were embrasures of rusted iron embedded in the thick concrete walls. He now realized where he was. He was inside the bunker.

Raspberry and blackberry brambles, shrunken from lack of light, lay twisted over the uneven floor. The walls were painted in a blackish hue. In a band of sunlight falling on the concrete wall he glimpsed a picture of a herd of animals, perhaps deer, as if children had drawn it. It looked just like those prehistoric drawings found on the walls of caves . . .

The corridor curved twice before he came to the exit. He couldn't go outside right away as the sun's glare caused his eyes excruciating pain. How long had he been inside for light to become so aggressive? He squinted like a nocturnal animal violently awoken. What day was it? It might even be a different season, he thought. It was wet, had probably rained, and the sun was shining through tattered clouds. He perceived the surrounding sounds with an acute, almost painful clarity. He could distinguish the rustling legs of an insect from the faint crackle produced by a bird stretching out its wings in the branches of a spruce. He heard the hissing tongue of a snake, sliding its slick body through the grass. A light breeze occasionally brushed the treetops. He could hear distinctly the moments of contact between any two leaves on any tree he locked in on. An unbelievably vibrant world of sound.

It was the same with odors. The amorphous aroma of forest grass, lichens, bark, and mushrooms had suddenly fractured into thousands of discrete, independent, precise perceptions. He spent a long time just randomly skimming all that diversity. After a while he managed to identify the exact positions of every living being within a wide radius. He knew where belladonna and wormwood were growing, where hidden underground was a truffle the size of a fist. If he'd had a rifle, he could've bagged a roe deer in seconds — he detected its odor so intensely at forty meters that it seemed his nose was plunged right into its fur. He was experiencing a bizarre sensation of absolute orientation in space.

He finally took a look around, but it didn't help much. He couldn't look at the sky. His eyes were still watering. He had to keep squinting and blinking as if a stubborn grain of dust was lodged under his eyelids. They burned and stung. So he relied on his other senses. And they led him securely through the forest.

He reached the creek. It had swelled with water to nearly twice its normal breadth. He washed off the dried mud that coated his skin. Something like paint was on his face. Although turbid, he noticed the water turn red when he splashed his face. His clothing was torn and soiled. He found a few deep cuts and several small abrasions and bruises on his body. In disgust he flushed several small worms from a wound. Maggots no doubt. His fingers opened up his lacerated skin in the muddy water. The wound snarled at him, and his lips unconsciously mimicked its grimace.

He opened the gate and walked through the yard. Suddenly a

vicious sorrow seized him. Kristýna. It sliced into him cleanly and to the quick. Something on the left side of his chest lurched. He swallowed. The door was locked. He'd lost the key somewhere. He circled the house a few times. He eventually broke a window, pushing shards from the frame with his hand protected by his sleeve and turning the handle from the inside. He crawled in. Everything was just as he'd left it. The chill of a country cottage. Fetid water in the sink. A plate on the table. The stench of mushrooms.

He bathed. He shaved and clipped his cracked nails. The more severe wounds he disinfected with iodine and bandaged. Hunger. He searched the pantry. He found two rolls, hard as rock. He filled a glass with water and soaked them. He picked up the telephone. Silence. It was dead. They'd cut it off. He walked over to the light switch. The electricity had also been disconnected. Strange. The bathroom had no window. He'd bathed in the dark as it hadn't occurred to him to light a lamp.

He took a tin box from the cupboard, opened it, and pocketed all the money inside. He put on clean clothes. Suddenly he realized he was having trouble breathing. Every breath flooded him with sharp, stabbing pain. He'd felt it since the moment he'd woken up, but was only now fully conscious of it. He recalled the pink stone that had been placed inside him in his dream. He decided to go to the hospital. Have his chest X-rayed or something. He had to make sure.

He climbed back out the window. The sky had grown overcast, which was much easier on his eyes. It started to drizzle. In the village they all looked at him as if he were an apparition. He waited for the bus. He spoke with no one. He didn't respond to anyone talking to him. Someone told him the police were looking for him. He said nothing. He stared at roots warping the asphalt at the bus stop. He heard every word being whispered about him. He smelled cheap cologne. Old sweat dried in the underarms of shirts. Onions someone had probably eaten for breakfast. Nicotine saliva spat in the dust. Last night's booze. In the bus he sat apart from the others.

He walked through town in a trance. Through the rumble of machines and roar of people, the clatter of shop shutters being pulled down, a child's cry, the shaking of a rattle, and a mother's hideous grimace that should have been a smile. Through the stammering of a jackhammer breaking up the sidewalk, the street, and Andrei's brain. Through the sucking of each drag off hundreds of cigarettes pinched between the fingers of assorted folks at the bus stop and main square as they imbibed the cancer from them.

That's it, flashed through his mind.

Andrei stopped at a newspaper stand, he had to light up, too. He closed his eyes and took a drag on the cigarette. Smoke flowed into him and produced incredible pain. It was like inhaling thistle. What the fuck, he coughed. He felt his whole chest ignite. He tossed the cigarette to the ground. Enveloped in the noise of the street, he continued on his way. The opening of a window. Words. Everywhere. In apartments, on sidewalks, on television. The hysterical squawk of radios. The scrape of a shovel's tongue licking up dirt in a ditch. He couldn't endure it anymore. With his teeth he tore a strip from his shirt, ripped it in half, rolled both pieces into small balls, and stuffed them into his ears. It helped a little.

He was still assailed by odor. The odor of sparks leaping from the crunch of a pickaxe. The odor of everything. The constant odor of bodies in town. The odor of dried up kisses on the neck of a passing man. The odor of blood from a bitten tongue in a school girl's mouth. The odor of sweaty hands on the stair railing at the hospital entrance. And ultimately the cold odor of disinfectant in the hospital corridors.

Finally quiet.

He removed the plugs from his ears. Cool floors covered in white linoleum. Cool, refreshing walls with faded posters of strange medications, and a cough somewhere on another floor. A cool reception from the nurse in the waiting room.

Before his turn came, he asked where he could find the doctor he'd spoken with the night Kristýna had died. The doctor wasn't at the hospital, but his assistant was. Andrei introduced himself to him with a fake name as Nina's relative. He informed Andrei that Nina had survived the poisoning and was currently being treated in a psychiatric hospital. He wrote the address on a piece of paper. Nina's husband was reported missing. Andrei thanked him.

When his turn came to see the doctor, Andrei explained that he'd been having difficulty breathing and that he wanted to find out why. They gave him a routine checkup and then sent him for an examination. And then another. They did blood tests, they X-rayed his lungs. He waited for hours in the corridor for the test results. They finally called him in and informed him that he had a tumor the size of an egg below his left lung. It was impossible to remove it since it was already too big.

"To be honest," the doctor nodded for him to sit down, "you've got about a month to live, two at most. I'm sorry."

•

We ride through small towns and villages near the border
in places where language is corrupted
where words we know end

The bus is near empty
the world flies past in fog

sleeping bodies exhale water
onto cold windows
the last night bus
tomorrow the glass will retain
greasy hair prints

We pass an abandoned concrete gatehouse
heaps of iron covered in moss
repositories of rust and stale air
a dog's eyes shine behind the fence
old jaws
teeth poisonous like the plants
growing around the corrugated tin
the days always the same
black with dust from the road
a fenced warehouse corridor
wearily crisscrossing
keeping guard in the rain
rust, wire, tin, and weeds

We are riding into a void
fields undulate outside
dirt the color of inner eyelids
a rhythm within
a principle
a perfect code producing black cells in lungs
the body ceasing to be whole

A film has coated my eyes
I watch the surface from underneath
out the windshield

beyond the oscillation of the wipers
a red fiber of brake lights stretches out
veering

Upon the milky surface of breath condensed on glass
my sleeve uncovered a cold piece of darkness
wet tree trunks sometimes flicker in

We ride along the border
I listen to a dead musician sing
on the driver's radio

•

The psychiatric hospital was formerly a chateau. Actually, it was
more a manor house with a series of decorative columns and friezes
that somewhat resembled a chateau. Its dilapidated façade was partially overgrown with ivy. The stone railings, window ledges, and
sills were crumbling. In many places the plaster was bubbling from
dampness, or even flaking off completely. The grounds around the
building were fairly spacious, enclosed by a high fence. Several
asphalt walkways, lined with yew and juniper bushes, crisscrossed
and led to the different corners of the garden. Over the paths hung
massive shadows cast by branches of old overgrown spruces.

Benches were scattered throughout the garden. The whole of it
created an uneasy calm. It was impossible not to think about the
endlessly repeating, regular walks along the same paths of the
quiet garden: once between breakfast and lunch, then between
afternoon medication and dinner, and one between dinner and
lights-out. All these places seemed to be without time. Only the
slow, bloodless shuffling of feet.

The same timelessness was inside the building. Contained between swinging glass doors, above floors of white, blue, and gray tiles, beneath high ceilings decorated with deteriorating moldings, on foot-worn granite stairways, behind a quivering film of rain bordered by the window frame.

He requested a visit at the reception desk.

"Name?" an old woman looked at him through her glasses and the glass of the reception desk.

"Andrei Březinka."

She wrote.

"That's . . . like Birkenau, the concentration camp, right?"

"Yeah."

He waited and listened as the rustle of turned pages echoed through the vestibule. He got the room number, but he still had to wait half an hour because it was lunchtime. He sat down on a bench opposite the reception window. The old woman assiduously fit letters into crossword squares. She occasionally stole a glance at him over the rim of her glasses. From the rustle and scratch of the pencil on paper, he perceived her individual strokes and interpreted the shapes of the letters she was writing to compose the individual words. He was fairly sure he would solve the puzzle before her, but he had to leave because the big hand on the square wall clock had finally arrived at the proper position.

Nina didn't speak to him even once. He, too, said nothing. She looked tired, her facial features had withered. She was all pale. Thinner. Her hair was strangely cut, tied up with an elastic band. She was still beautiful. Maybe even more beautiful than before. Her eyes were swimming. He couldn't tell whether she was suppressing tears or still numbed by medication. She'd been placed alone in a double room. They sat next to each other on the bed, covered in plastic. They watched the rain. It was just past noon, but outside the sky, heavy with clouds, was already growing dim as if evening were coming on. He held her firmly by the hand. A bitter taste in his mouth, he had to breathe it out, because he was on the verge of tears. He had no idea what to do next. Absolute emptiness. He could hear steps in the corridor through the door. An icy rod full of white light jangled on the ceiling. He sank deeper and deeper into the anxiety of the moment.

His gaze slipped down the nylon curtains to the radiator, inspecting all of its twists and turns before finally resting on a photo leaning against a flowerpot on the table by the window. Next to the photo was a key. Nothing else was on the bare plywood surface. The photo was of a house, an old cottage like somewhere in a Moravian village. It stood in a spacious yard with fields and a pine forest spreading out behind it. Something in Polish was written in marker at the bottom. The plant in the pot was strange, exotic. Maybe an orchid.

So Kryštof had been here. It stung him, but he said nothing. He decided he had to find him. He had to see him. He didn't know exactly what he wanted to do, to say, but he felt there was no other alternative.

He stood. He kissed Nina on the cheek. She lowered her head, and he stood a moment longer in the door, indecisive, waiting to see if she'd say something, if the ice would break.

Only the rattle of rain on the windowsill.

He turned and left.

•

The sky looked like dirty dishwater. It seemed the rain would never let up. The drainage ditch running through the town could normally be stepped over with no problem in most places, but now a massive muddy current was raging through it and on the verge of overflowing. Noxious clouds, distended like a celestial inflammation, touched the roofs of the tallest buildings. The rain they unleashed without respite upon the earth no longer found any ground to saturate. A nervous energy reigned over the town.

Andrei, drenched to the bone, took shelter in the train station. An unusually large number of people were waiting. Every bench was occupied. Countless travelers were sitting on their luggage or on the bare ground. Together they produced a buzzing chorus filling the glass-roofed hall. Andrei plugged his ears again.

Children in colorful nylon anoraks frolicked among faces stupefied by the long wait. A family locked in a huddle around their angry father ate bread and salami. The head of an elderly man drowsing sank onto the shoulder of a girl sitting next to him on a bench. She interrupted her conversation with her friend to shake him off and glare at him with undisguised disgust. Two lovers took a break from kissing and out of boredom began chatting about nothing.

A television blared in the station snack bar. The news was on. A crowd of people were crammed inside working on getting drunk. A guy holding a beer glass slipped through the throng in front of the entrance and sat down in front of the glass display case. Although smoking wasn't allowed in the station, the snack bar was an exception. The unshaven faces of men floated in the gray air.

Each traveler would glance at the timetable every few seconds. Most of the trains were delayed by more than an hour. One was even five and a half hours behind. At the moment Andrei looked at the schedule, a half hour was tacked on to several of the connections, triggering a wave of sighs, tut-tutting, and head shaking throughout the hall.

Andrei approached the counter and asked when the next train to Prague was leaving.

"Now it's supposed to depart at 4:31 p.m. The next express at 6:36 p.m." The ticket lady said and apologetically added with a shrug of her shoulders, "but you certainly shouldn't count on it, water's torn up the tracks at Volary and Kralupy is also washed out, so everything's all messed up. They're sending them through as fast as they can . . ."

"Fine. So, one ticket to Masaryk Station. I'll wait." He searched his pockets for money.

"Masaryk is closed. Because of Karlín, you know. Everything's being routed to Prague Main Station."

"What do you mean because of Karlín?" he said, confused.

She looked at him inquisitively through the glass.

"Well, because it's underwater."

"What?"

"It's underwater, it's been flooded. Floods." She emphasized and smiled. "Don't you have a television, or something?"

"No." He frowned. "Okay, one to the main station."

He dove into in the reeking snack bar. He waded through a horde of people sitting or standing around four tables and reached the beer tap. The clatter of glass, the hollow bumping of beer glasses being rinsed. He ordered a beer and a vodka. One large and one small smack on the wet stainless-steel counter. He lit a cigarette and inhaled gingerly. Everything seemed alright. When he honed in on the surrounding roar and distinguished individual voices in it, he realized no one was speaking about anything but the floods. An old guy in overalls was talking about how the water had taken his cottage.

"Yesterday my neighbor and I watched from a hill as my whole roof got pulled clean off . . . It bumped into his house and probably saved it 'cause it deflected the water like a breaker, know what I mean," he said. "So we got drunk, and well, I've been drunk since. He was happy as a fool laughing at me the whole time. What an ass." He gulped down his beer.

Another table with another stubbly mouth swaying above a beer-stained tablecloth embroidered with a floral pattern.

"It was hauling off whole trees. Totally flooded the fields and road. When I was coming back they were about to close the bridge. I might've been the last one across. Then it was washed away."

And others . . .

"My old lady does nothing but stare at the TV, she's all fired up about it. Well, it's on day and night, nonstop. The reports get her all wound up. All those people standing around in some mess saying where their kitchen used to be, living room, there was a bedroom over here and on and on."

. . .

"I totally forgot about them in all the confusion. They stayed locked in there. So, yeah. But they wouldn't have gotten out alive anyway. They weren't gonna just swim away. And what would I be doing now with eighteen rabbits anyhow, right?"

. . .

"Yep, we're sittin' pretty. We live right below the forest, where you make the turn at the Lukeš place, up the hill. Right, right, that's it. All the way up the hill. So I don't have to give a fuck about it."

. . .

"No, I'm going to some old gal's place in Prague. She's all worried about some fucking potatoes. Her cellar's flooded. So at least I'll get to see what's all been washed away there."

The television suspended from the ceiling in a corner above the taps was more or less repeating the same.

Andrei sat in a vacated seat at one of the tables. From here he could also hear the announcements of train arrivals. It was the only time the noise of the snack bar quieted as everyone tried to understand the crackly voice coming from the loudspeakers. After each announcement several people tossed back the remains of their alcohol, eyes bulging, paid hurriedly, and rushed off to the platforms.

His hand slid along the wet glass. He drank quickly. A motionless cloud of smoke clung to the ceiling. They were all inhaling it. Heavy air was passed from lungs to lungs by every person in the room. Nothing fresh. A slut, it occurred to him. Air that puts out for everyone. He breathed the breath of the station attendant sitting across from him. The same breath had recently traveled through the nostrils of the elderly man whose roof had been taken by the water, through several tattooed young guys who, based on their general appearance, made their livings as taxi drivers, through a scrawny man squeezed in by the door, wearing a thin mustache and a nylon jacket, filling himself with a glass of rum.

He watched the movement of the gray tendrils forming at the end of his cigarette. The movement of jaws talking about the river. The beer tasted like the soap used to wash the glasses. The barman was doing a lousy job of it anyway because when held against the light the imprint of greasy lips was clearly visible on the rim of the glass. Over it all thundered the furious punching of buttons on two gambling machines at the door that every so often would emit an electric whinny like a mutilated county fair.

"On track three, boarding for the delayed express train to Česká Třebová, Ústí nad Orlicí, Choceň, Pardubice Main Station, Přelouč, Kolín, Prague-Libeň, Prague Main Station." The announcement was momentarily drowned out by the skidding of bar stools across the floor: ". . . the restaurant car and storage car are located at the back of the train. We apologize for the delay."

Andrei rose. He was momentarily off balance, so put out his cigarette in the ashtray more forcefully than he'd intended.

While locating the left sleeve of his sweater, he blankly stared at a spot on the table plastered in a paper mash of wet beer coasters.

Moments later, he was sitting in the acrid odor of the train's imitation-leather seats. Rain fell tirelessly on the iron rails, the switches, and the decommissioned freight cars.

•

It's strange that a person can't go without sleep. You can die quicker from extreme wakefulness than from hunger. If the body goes too long without getting to the dream state, it dies. If thinking is too rational too long, it dies. Experiences in dreams are in no way less real than in waking life. Senses function the same in both cases: all tastes, touches, smells, and other perceptions are fully registered. When awake, we don't understand the logic of dreams, and in dreams the laws and rules of our waking state don't apply. Just as we often cannot clearly and exactly remember most events in dreams, in sleep we remember very little of when we weren't asleep. These are the two worlds our bodies inhabit. Actually, just the brain and the senses. Two worlds tenuously connected by our memory, an intermediary so limited that it simultaneously serves as their starkest divide.

This is what Andrei was thinking when he awoke in the express train nearing the capital city, as he watched the dark landscape out the window, the silhouette of a tree, a pole, or crossing gates sometimes popping into view. He tried to explain the events of the past couple of days. Nothing made sense. He fell into a strange apathy. He couldn't at all understand the direction his life had taken. The pointlessness of going to Prague, God knows why he was fixated on it, it even bewildered him. What lay in store, what would happen there? What did he even want to do when he saw Kryštof? Kick his ass? Tell him he'd destroyed everything he'd been living for, something silly like that? Why? Darkness. Car lights at a train crossing. Why? In truth, nothing mattered to him. Nina, Kryštof, and Kristýna, his own diseased body, none of it.

On everything that is and was, I inscribe Nihil. Nothing. The hiss of the tracks and darkness.

Orange lamp light colored the foggy mist rising from the ground in the park that led from the train station. The color of the light was probably purposefully adjusted a long time until its tint matched the cigarette filters littering the grass and asphalt walkway, rendering them almost indiscernible, and thus the city saved on street cleaning.

It was half past two. The silent, sticky steps of several sleepless travelers went their separate ways along the wet paths. The cool of the dusty city air. The snap of opening umbrellas in the exits, like the frightened flight of a startled bird. The beating of crows' wings into the sky.

Night. Andrei mulled over what to do next. He suddenly felt desperately weak.

Kryštof, then?

No . . . not yet.

He didn't even have the strength to speak, let alone punch someone. He had to see him with a clear head. The whole thing was just ridiculous.

Go back . . . ?

Failed pitiful world. Worst of all possible. He paused in confusion at the edge of the park, scanned his surroundings indecisively for a moment, and finally started walking in the direction of Wenceslas Square.

The greatest concentration of Prague filth. The place where police officers, leaning on open car doors, wearily watch the movements of junkies and meth dealers. Where a group of Germans desperately search for prostitutes, asking passersby where they might be found. Where in food kiosks sausages fry nonstop, twenty-four hours a day, their stink filling the whole square, and thoughts of ambrosia and manna steal into the dreams of the homeless occupying all the benches. Where something is constantly being repaired underground. Work here doesn't stop even at night, judging by the shadows that sometimes flicker in the bright gaps of aluminum fencing surrounding the worksites. It is an ill quarter of the city, living independently of time of day or season of year.

Andrei ate some meaty junk he'd bought at one of the kiosks. A beggar slammed into him.

"Pardon me," the stink of soured wine wafted over him, "could you spare some change?" Eyes rheumy with disease obnoxiously stabbed into him. Andrei froze for a second, the whites of the guy's eyes were all spoiled, rancid.

"Fuck off, asshole!" he shoved him away.

He was sick to his stomach. He thought it might be a good idea for the municipality to collect this kind of refuse every night, mash them up in a press, and then use the mash as fertilizer for the trees in the parks . . .

He was ashamed of himself. He remembered the scent of the chapel where they would take him every Sunday when he was little. He turned into the quiet of a side street.

Marián! The idea suddenly came to him.

Definitely. He could sleep at his place. He tried to remember where he lived. It wasn't really that far. Fifteen minutes later he was pressing the doorbell. A serene street on a hill. A row of parked cars on each side. Absolute solace. Only the synchronized movements of blue light cast by televisions onto the ceilings of two apartments in the building opposite. Nothing. He rang again. He stood there a moment longer and rang one last time to be sure, then left.

He ducked into the closest nonstop bar he found and drank for as long as he could.

•

That night the great waters subsided
the city's embankments now covered by a blanket of mud
tree branches
dislodged cobblestones and debris from other places
the river bled into the streets
and receded
now it is quiet
after a single heartbeat of flood

I walk along the bank
dawn breaking
I'm tottering
in a world crooked with alcohol

I pause before the pools of detritus
water inert in them
out of reach of the current
in them glimmer fish
turned onto the wrong side skyward
I watch that buoyant, milky rocking
they bob in ripples formed by a wan wind

and again show their slender shanks
the color of bread mold
the water flips the blind gaze of fish moons

Cool August
the flood chased animals from the forests

The river brought grass, soil,
and varied plastic items
all now drying in bushes and treetops

Colorful sediment
undulates in cutoff streams
plastic bottles collide into each other
knocking as if in port
like scattered buoys
while a fisherman sleeps
streaks of light changing, shimmering on the surface
pulled in from the opposite bank
begin to disperse

Footfalls in his sleep
each step reverberating up his spine
thus the weight of a sleeping child
you carry in your arms to bed
as I now carry myself
through this faltering night
a night in whose darkness
a whole city perished along its banks

My hands are red from rust

shirt torn
I climbed over something old and metallic
I can't remember
I walk through a submerged city
unimaginable quiet here
the area cordoned off
I watch the horizon
dog blood rabid in my head
dog breath from vodka racing over the steppe inside me
I observe the vein of light before me

Where am I?
I am lost
under my feet something's silently subsiding
the horizon gently sways
and rotates into the vertical position

•

Andrei curled up into a ball. He was deluged with a wave of genuine
self-pity. It stung inside his nose, as tears began to well.
    Where am I?
    My God, where have I ended up?
    He crushed wet sand in his fist.
    What have we done? What have we done so terrible that You
dish out such punishment to us? To me and Nina! To Kristýna . . . !
    I obviously deserve it, I know . . .
    You can do it to me, but why them?
    Why Nina?
    Take this pain away from her and give it to me . . . !
    Give it to me . . .

I'll bear anything now!

Now I'm just a vessel for pain . . . Nothing more. I am the emptiest place in this miserable world . . .

Do You hear?!

. . . do You hear me?

I confess . . .

I confess to everything. I've acted shamefully . . .

To those who loved me . . . I betrayed their love. I was afraid to give myself to someone. I was afraid I'd lose it. I didn't want to risk . . . to risk that, again . . .

I confess. I'll confess to anything You want. I've lived badly. I've lived badly. Badly! I have lived in the worst way I could!

. . .

I want to change it. I'm asking You . . . I of You . . . I lie here in utter filth and beg: give me another chance! Please, let it be a dream. Let me wake up in the morning . . .

Uh . . .

. . .

But I tried! Bastard, I tried! I did what I could . . . Are You listening to me?

It was You who put this sadness in me, this loneliness, bitterness, hate, despair . . .

IT WAS YOU! . . .

What are we guilty of?

WHAT . . . ARE . . . WE . . . GUILTY . . . OF?

Do You hear?

Why have You abandoned us?

Why?!

. . .

You know what? Screw it . . . All of it! You've abandoned me. Now I . . . I am abandoning You. I'll destroy myself . . .

I, You . . .

He was disgusted with himself. There was nowhere to talk to. And no one. For a moment the devil walked in the flood debris attentively listening for Andrei to utter the words he intended in anger. But Andrei's eyelids abruptly and unexpectedly slammed shut, the motion rocking the world around him so that all at once he fell asleep.

•

That moment stretches out like a string of honey
blending all the rhythms inside
into a regular contact of the surface
everything slows
reverses
nestles into another body
the flight of a swan opens rings on water
clapping

The serenity of amniotic fluid
I rock
I am translucent
warm strings lead into me
outside they reach into me through the skin, smiling
they say my name
but I hear only thrumming
entranced by the regular pulsing of blood
and all the living movements inside
in the most beautiful music of the body
I am sleeping
in warm water

there never was anything
and emptiness is in all that follows
I am right now
a perfect fruit

A car driving past is heard through the walls
outside a street
but secluded silence here
dust whirls in the light
like tea leaves settling in a teapot
the light's the color of tea, too
from window to floor the slanted plank of evening
benches of polished wood here
and only a few people huddling in prayer
pigeons fly near the ceiling
their cooing and small talons heard
they are city birds
full of filth and flaws

I watch them
nearby, wondrous
lips moving without sound
exhaling God
imploring
or thanking
with closed eyes
I imagine her naked
I place my face on her warm skin
and listen to the sounds of the street in the church walls

I open my eyes in the bath

above me light and tile lines undulate
the enamel squeaks when I move
I cradle myself in those fish sounds
I'm hanging in tepid soapy water
I almost can't touch
rippled skin soaked white
so fragile and painful
the water gave me warmth
I have it in my body, my bones
I exhale
the surface rises at the other end
it's perfectly level, just balancing itself
a long stream hums inside
just like the blood in a head
and everything is spinning
spinning in tepid milt

The skin is bare
I gently rock
on the breath
in the body
street sounds in church walls
there never was anything
and emptiness is in all that follows
I am perfect
and you sleep
we breathe on each other
warmth slides along your belly
all the way to the hollow in the middle
in it a small knot of skin
I warily touch

it is almost unbelievable
and you, like me
sometime long ago
you incubated sleeping in another body
you were one with it
you hung among viscera
like a lush fruit
like me once
like an apple
you grew heavier
rushing toward separation
to the greatest injustice

You, too, left warmth and rhythm then
the hard clay of autumn tapped in the flesh
and you breathed in chill

The heart no longer sounds in a white room
that hurts the eyes
accustomed to water and darkness
everyone came screaming into foreign hands
and left alone forever
he was born
drenched in umbilical blood
forced to breathe air
with a knot in the body
separated from mother by a knife
with a scream
that meant hate
and helplessness

You smell foam in the crack
putrid aroma of cider
in an abandoned garden
apples mold and split open in the grass
in a dead orchard solstices spin
thirty years of my life
iron in a clapboard shack
garden tools covered in rust
stacks of wet walnut leaves
emit white smoke
full of water
the weight of milk

I hang in tepid water
my spine stretched out on the bottom
the enamel chiming
the surface weighs two masses of water
kilos of water from two sides
and above the water is smoke
flowing in through the window from the garden

I open my eyes
in the center of your belly a scar
a small knot
the sign of your solitude
a reminder
blood is pounding
already so powerfully it starts to hurt
water twisted the skin into tiny flowers
macerated on fingers
I open up

the surface weighs
kilos of dead water
the heart no longer sounds in a white room
and everything
everything returns
inward
into another body
outside they say my name
but I hear only humming
a single sound
the length of a string of honey
my name is outside
exchanged for water
for a pulse
that hurts
that can no longer endure
it claps
like a dropped fish mincing itself
on paving stones beneath a carp tub
like rings opening on the surface of water
beneath a swan's flight
on the river and throughout the valley
beating
white
wings

●

Waking up.

    Machines. Clumps of moist sand slap against the water as they slide down from a serrated shovel. The sky opens in Andrei's eye.

The huge morning sky, with all its pain, pries open the fissure between his lids.

Light in the sky. Clear again after so long. In it the first riparian birds cry and wheel in flight, describing ever deeper arcs. Heavier despite the air in their hollow bones. They fade from Andrei's tired vision in unbroken gull-colored lines. They swallow their own shouts, choked squalls reverberating off the windowpanes of riverside houses. They coolly circle the destroyed city, eating from the detritus the remains of what was once alive.

A light went out on the opposite bank. Grit next to his hand scattered by a yawn and merged with the glare from the sky, the water's surface, and a gull, and the sound in his head stilled the world. Everything was suddenly iridescent like the debris on the river.

For a while he breathed in the aroma of the wet sand and listened to the sound of the water, reminding him of the din of a construction site. He opened his eyes again. He felt ill. His head was full of blood. He was lying awkwardly at a downward angle. He ran his tongue along the roof of his mouth and found a sore spot: in the middle of the wrinkled roof, its surface rippled like a walnut shell, hung a small sharp sliver of flesh. He considered for a moment why these mysterious abrasions always appeared when he woke up. He felt sand in his teeth. He bit down and scraped enamel.

He wasn't quite sure where he'd woken up. He recalled several things from the night before. Fish bellies in debris on the bank. Empty streets full of mud. Dead lamps hanging above the abandoned city. Light on the horizon. Dawn. He realized he couldn't have slept for more than two hours because the sun was just coming up, and the thought amplified his overwhelming fatigue and nausea. His body used all the energy gained in sleep to sober up at least a little. He had a round pain in his belly, somewhere to the left of his stomach. An acrid stench in his nostrils and under his tongue. The needles in his lungs had returned, tiny sutures stitching up his flesh with his every breath, stitching up his tissue with thread spun from cancer cells. He tried to breathe as shallowly as he could.

He attempted to sit up, but immediately thudded back onto the sand as the blood that had accumulated in the upper half of his body while sleeping instantly produced sparks and blackness when he'd raised up, flooding his eyes, blinding him, stinging his fingertips, and sweetly, almost euphorically, spinning him in a vortex of vertigo. He had to lie down again and wait for his circulation to return to its normal state of equilibrium.

Somewhere behind him machines were working in the water. They were opening the earth on the riverbank. An iron digger scraped loudly over rocks.

As soon as the water receded, people began feverishly to repair the city.

The motor of a backhoe.

The hissing of hydraulics.

He got up, beat the sand from his clothing, brushing the dried and wet mud off his pants. It didn't help much.

As he was leaving, the quizzical stares of the workmen in their reflective vests trailed after him. One of them was measuring something in the air between his hands, speaking to a colleague, and when he noticed Andrei, his eyes under the plastic visor of his hard hat latched onto Andrei's suspicious figure and dourly moved with it until it had vanished among the apartment buildings. Andrei wished he could shoo the glance with his hand, as he would an annoying bug. He felt it burning uncomfortably into his back and neck. He finally walked into emptiness around a corner, where he was only followed by the echoes of motors and the thundering of metal diggers excavating mud and rocks.

He set off toward the inhabited part of the city.

The empty streets guided him. They directed him without his having to think. The water had receded. His tired body moved slowly past in darkened shop windows. Closed. Everything was closed. Everyone was inside. In buildings beyond the water's border. The streets were drained fishponds. Everything smelled of the river, and a multitude of fish moons motionlessly directed their gazes heavenward.

He froze.

"Hey, stop!" someone shouted behind him.

He turned around. Two guys in black pants and jackets. Security guards.

He stopped.

They walked up to him, and one of them grabbed his sweater.

"What were you looking for over there?"

"Nothing."

"Ok, ok . . ." his voice lingered, "right, nothing. What's your name?"

"Excuse me?"

"Your name, fuckwad!"

"Andrei Holocaust . . . Please take your hands off me!"

"Do you think we're really that stupid? Show us what you got on you. Where's the loot?" They started to go through his pockets. "So whatcha steal, asshole?"

"What the fuck are you talking about?" He tore himself away.

"So you're just gonna cause problems, is that it? Don't think I didn't see you over there!" he barked in his face.

"You're mistaking me for someone else. I didn't steal anything. I don't know . . . just leave me the fuck alone!" He forced their hands away again and turned to leave, but one of the guards grabbed him and thrust him against the damp reeking wall of a building.

Andrei lost it. He shoved his hand under the guy's neck and squeezed until his eyes bulged with pain. He then bounced off the wall while managing to hold the guard at arm's length.

"Piece of shit!" he heard over his left side. The second guard pulled out his tonfa, which till then had been swinging at his waist, cocked it back, and brought it down on the shoulder of Andrei's arm that had the first guard's Adam's apple in its grip. He let go. Burning pain shot through his shoulder muscle and into his head. His knees buckled. His vision darkened with adrenaline. His jaws clenched in rage, anxiety, and desperation. All the moments of helplessness in his life surged through his head. And then something happened that horrified even him.

The guard raised his arm to hit him again. Andrei roared and caught the tonfa in his hand before it fell. It smacked his palm. He held it firmly, twisted it, and dislocated the man's wrist. Then, incredibly, he struck the guard in the face four times in quick succession with the extended end of the hilt. Andrei broke his cheek bone, knocked out his front teeth, and shattered his nose. In a fraction of a second, he was aware of all the weak points in the guard's body. He saw his skeleton, as if it were phosphorescent through his black uniform. He saw the colored blood and all the other liquids inside the man. He exactly perceived the tension points of his heart and all the other organs around it. He saw three or four horrific possibilities for where to strike him next. He knew exactly how to kill him instantly.

All of this transpired in less than two seconds. Scared and confused, Andrei dropped the tonfa. The guard collapsed in the mud. Blood was spurting from his face, burbling as he tried to breathe.

He groaned softly, almost childlike, his wary sobbing broken by a strange hiss. He still held his weapon in his contorted hand. Frozen, the second guard looked at his partner. Andrei, too, stood dumbstruck for a moment, then turned quickly and walked off in a random direction as if in a trance. He couldn't begin to fathom what had happened. His surroundings swung in the rhythm of his step. Behind him he heard the guard swallowing blood. Andrei broke into a run.

•

Marián tossed his cigarette butt into the street and before walking to the entrance door watched as it rolled along the curb and eventually fell into a crack between the original cobblestones peeking out under the broken asphalt. He was holding a plastic bag full of food and vegetables, a newspaper under his arm. A ring of keys jingled as he pulled it out of his pocket. He turned and examined the keys with one hand until he selected one, and secured it between his thumb and index finger. As soon as he extended his hand and inserted the key into the lock and heard the familiar, reassuring click of metal teeth, the click of the lock, and tinkle of wire mesh glass, as his foot opened the door into the entry full of cellar smell, he stopped dead.

"Holy shit." He flinched in surprise when he raised his eyes and saw Andrei leaning against the ceramic tiled wall beside the set of doorbells.

"Christ, you scared me," he laughed with almost exaggerated relief. "Where the hell did you come from? What've you been up to?" He noticed Andrei's clothing. Andrei peeled himself off the wall and squeezed the hand Marián extended.

"Well, look, I'll tell you later. Can I come in?"

"Of course you can. Can you take this for me?" He handed him the bag and called the elevator.

Marián's apartment was full of flowers. He had a large balcony encased in glass that served as his greenhouse. He regulated the moisture and heated it in winter. He'd laid down a layer of soil and brought some wood inside, which rotted, and out of that rot spectacular flowers grew. Andrei examined everything with curiosity, and Marián supplied him with commentary, adding flourishes of detail, description, and points of interest for each plant, all of which Andrei forgot instantaneously.

He asked if he could take a shower. Marián loaned him some clothes. Clean pants, a T-shirt and sweatshirt. They had a bite to eat. They sat at the kitchen table and sipped black coffee, dispelling sleep with the blackness from white mugs. Andrei told him about Kristýna. They spent a moment in heavy silence.

"How's the flooding been at your place? Did it wash you away?" Marián asked to break the uncomfortable silence.

"No worries, we're almost in the hills. It's like nothing happened."

"It's been absolutely insane here . . . But it could've been expected. It rained like crazy for a whole month. And then it came roaring in and half the city was flooded. A large part of the subway is underwater . . ." Marián sipped coffee and continued. Andrei observed his face. He looked very tired, too. Marián had brown skin. His mother was Romany, but he looked more Italian or Greek. His hair was black and wavy, and stuck out from his head in all directions. "And they counted on the subway serving as a shelter from the flood wave if the Vltava's cascade of dams didn't hold. I mean everyone would totally be screaming in there. And then we probably wouldn't even be sitting here because the water'd be all the way up to the windows."

He offered Andrei a cigarette. They lit up. Andrei looked out the window. The sky was gray, expressionless, motionless, void of any interesting feature. It was the perfect reflection of his thoughts. A flawless illustration.

"And at the zoo they had to shoot some hippos or elephants, or something, because they would've drowned otherwise."

"Seriously?"

"Then a sea lion escaped, swam out down the river. It died Tuesday morning in Germany. It was a huge tragedy on TV."

They laughed. Marián talked tirelessly. He explained how high the water had reached in different places, about Stromovka Park, Zbraslav, Karlín, about everything the flood had destroyed downtown, he presented several theories about why the subway had flooded. He spoke of old corridors and shafts running under the whole of Prague, most likely for military purposes, under Charles Square he said there was even a subterranean emergency hospital, to be used if war ever broke out. "It's possible," he speculated passionately, "that water got into some of those places. They also say that when the communists built it they cut corners and never completely resolved the system of closures and door seals."

Andrei listened to all of it for a while with no real interest, and at the first convenient opportunity he asked about Kryštof. Just if he was in town, and that he'd like to see him. This produced a change in Marián's face.

"It'd probably be better not to even start talking about fucking Kryštof," he said, suddenly nervous. Andrei looked at him with curiosity. "I'd like to know where he is, too," he let slip out.

"What . . . did something happen?" he moved his chair closer to the table.

Marián waved his hand. Silence.

Andrei watched him closely.

The silence lasted a moment longer. He put his mug on the table. It knocked against the wood. He scratched the stubble on his face.

"Yeah," he hesitated, "I guess it'd be good for you to know anyway," Marián said reluctantly. "It likely has nothing to do with you, but who knows." He gazed in thought somewhere toward the wall.

"It's just that this one deal is a little . . . unusual. A few days ago Kryštof arrived, I mean, should have arrived, from Japan. I haven't seen him and I don't even want to see him now, so . . . but let's start from the beginning."

Marián began explaining how he and Kryštof had been making a living for the last seven years. Because he trusted him, he said, he revealed in rough outline the whole mechanism of the black-market flower trade.

"Remember when we were in St. Petersburg? You were looking for your relative, or someone," Marián began. He spoke nervously, rapidly, stuttering. He obviously had a lot to say, but at the same time he hesitated over every sentence as if he wasn't sure what he could and couldn't tell Andrei.

"Yeah . . ."

"Well, I was there to close this deal. A wealthy collector. You seriously wouldn't believe the luxury he lived in. Super cool design. Spacious sparse rooms, an angular armchair here and there or some other clean, geometrical furniture. And various inconspicuous, minimalistic flower arrangements. But the flowers! Jewels . . . absolutely the most endangered species. I knew some of them only from black and white photos with the 'extinct' tag printed over them. This was no gardener, understand. No stuffy greenhouse full of tropical stink. Each and every flower required special care, a specially created environment behind glass. Some of them were just in tall glass cylinders. Amazing . . ."

A short, nervous pause. He reached for his cigarettes. Sparked the lighter. A brief deliberation. Would he really tell Andrei? The question could be read on his face. But at the same time he clearly needed to say something, it was obvious from the start that he needed to get something off his chest. Something was suffocating him. He was afraid of something. He breathed in and out.

"Well, and he was so smooth. A man of around fifty, maybe older. In an elegant suit, smoking a cigarette, and before he finished smoking it, his ashtray was changed three times . . . There were three other guys in the room. Two of them real goons. Bodyguards . . . Well, and then finally: he wanted a flower. I'd never heard of it before . . . He explained the situation very quickly, clearly and to the point. But first he gave me his price . . . I almost had a heart attack. So at that point I was pretty sure it was something real shady. I said, this isn't a job for us. But when I told Kryštof, he felt differently about it . . . And he agreed to go get the flower from Japan. I can't imagine where the guy got such detailed information, but he gave me the exact address of where to find it. He showed me a map of Tokyo with the location of an estate belonging to an impoverished noble family with a garden and that flower. The last of its kind, the only specimen . . . right? Standard theft. He simply wanted us to steal it. I told him I couldn't make a decision without Kryštof, so we agreed I'd call him a week later, and I got the hell out of there. I couldn't get mixed up in stuff like that, you know. The kind of money he was willing to pay, it scared me . . ."

"And so Kryštof went alone . . ."

"Yeah. I was pretty surprised. But he had some plans. I don't know what. I think he saw it as his last job . . . that kind. Then he'd just walk away after it was over. He got an advance and bought a house in Poland, on the coast. He also recently mentioned a couple of times that he has a girl. Finally the right one, he told me . . ." He laughed. "So God knows what he has up his sleeve."

Andrei's throat seized up. The psychiatric hospital, he thought. The photo on Nina's table . . .

"Yeah?" he responded weakly, sounding more like a frog. But Marián seemed not to notice and continued his story.

"So Kryštof left ten days ago. He had three contacts in Europe where he could deliver the flower. Vienna, where he flew out of and should have flown back to, Prague, and Wrocław. He didn't get a visa to Russia, but you already know that. I have no clue what happened in Japan except that he has the flower. But now, the most important thing." Marián bit his lip and leaned in closer to Andrei.

"He's only spoken with me once the entire time for security reasons. He's already in Europe. He was totally stressed out. He told me to pay close attention to the people around me, that I better not go outside much and so on. It seems someone from Tokyo's after him. Someone just keeps following him. Not the police or anything like that. For sure it's someone sent by that noble family, but Kryštof still doesn't know. Actually, he doesn't know anything at all. I think he's completely unaware of what he's gotten himself into. I have to tell him somehow. I found something out. The flower was something like the family jewels. Pretty unusual heritage, but still. I think we were kept in the dark about it on purpose, know what I mean? It has to be someone from Japan. Kryštof's return flight was overnight through Amsterdam. I don't know why. He called me from there. Someone from the St. Petersburg employer contacted him, saying he shouldn't go to Vienna under any circumstances, seems their guy there is, they said . . . he's dead. Someone took him out. Quite brutally . . . Kryštof mainly said the person following him is consciously working against the plan. So it's possible he's going after everyone involved to get information. That means I'm definitely not a hundred percent safe either . . . And considering the killer knew one of the handoff points was

Vienna, he probably knows, or tortured it out of the Vienna contact, that Prague is the next stop . . . So it's not out of the question that he's here somewhere already. I'd say it's almost certain . . ."

Marián was in a state by now. He fidgeted nervously with the lighter, flipping it over and over between his fingers. "And something very strange happened to me. Something really, really weird. Two days ago. I only ran across the street to the shop for cigarettes. It was already dark. I came out, stood in front of the shop, lit up, and started right back home. And suddenly someone came out of the alley and grabbed me. I almost shit myself because I'd been expecting something for several days. But it was some homeless guy, stinky, filthy, old, but surprisingly strong. He tackled me to the ground. I tried to get him off me but his grip on my throat was like steel. I never would've thought . . . He had those reddish sores on his face that people like this usually get from booze. He drove me to the sidewalk with one hand while the other reached into the pocket of his greasy jacket and pulled out a photo. A photo of me! He checked the resemblance and gave me an ugly look with that disgusting face of his and then said something in English! Perfect English! "Pleased to meet you, Mister Marian Rotko." I screamed at him to tell me what he wanted. I made one more useless attempt to throw him off me . . . He forced me back to the ground. So I said to myself, now I'm definitely fucked . . . And at that moment a police car pulled up by the sidewalk, thank God. The homeless guy jumped off and disappeared into the shadows of the alley he'd crawled out of. One of the cops took off running after him. The other one stayed with me. Some people were standing around, I hadn't noticed them at all before. They slowly started to walk away. I felt like bashing their faces in — not one of them tried to help me! They just stood in front of the shop gawping. I told the police I wouldn't file a report. I didn't want the police to start poking around on top of everything else. But the cop said no, that it had to be reported, mumbled something about a mugging and so on. So he wrote it down. I somehow talked my way through it and ran home." Marián was quiet. He extinguished his cigarette and immediately lit another. He continued in a quieter tone, "I don't get it. I have no idea what that was all about. Look, Andrei, recently I've been really . . . scared shitless. Now that you know what's been going on, you should also be careful. I mean, you're friends with Kryštof, someone might be looking for you, too. Though I doubt . . . anyway, just . . . watch your step. And I definitely do not recommend making contact with Kryštof in any way now. He's the center of the whole thing. He has the flower . . ."

"I have to see him," Andrei said decisively. "This stuff is your problem. I have to see Kryštof no matter what."

Marián shook his head and shrugged. He got up from the table and walked into the hall. He came back and placed two keys on a metal ring in front of Andrei.

"If that's what you want, here are the keys to his apartment, you can wait for him . . . Kryštof's probably in Prague by now. And if he isn't, he'll be here soon. If you see him, tell him to stay away from me for a while. And please," he took an envelope out of a drawer, already stamped and addressed, "give him this. I wrote his address here," he pointed with his finger. "You'll have to take the tram, the subway's closed."

When they said goodbye, Andrei noticed that Marián had a scar on his neck, just above his collarbone.

When he saw Andrei looking at it, Marian said, "yeah, that's from Bolivia, a long time ago. I'll tell you next time." He smiled. "It was good to see you."

"You, too. And thanks . . ."

•

Down into the city
Andrei kills his days like boys a dog
according to the Asian calendar
it is the year of the mulatto
everything connects and intertwines
moldy air wafts from cellars
and the face up there
with a scar on tea-colored skin
before dawn
drunk
saw fish bellies
found out where to go
and air howls below
he approaches

Leaning against the glass in the tram
thinking about himself
telling himself
not much time left
I only wish to be empty now
that is my path
rid myself of all names
rid myself of things as I know them
as anyone knows them
I return to the core
because everything begins there
this world isn't external, it's only through me
I give form to people
and to all the words they say

I give color and odor to the wet evening sidewalk
to the meadow as it lies soft in thaw
to the pieces of snow melting in its matted grass

I give touch and meaning to everything
moving around my body
I give taste to the saliva in foreign mouths
and the bruised brown flesh
all of it is inside
there is no friendship or love
each thing has thousands of forms
constantly spinning
at every moment possible to see it differently
every thing is in motion
this massive opaque flow carries me with it
like a river at the beginning of spring carrying away dirt
it is everywhere around me
I give it many names
many words and every one is false and unnecessary
my life

He jerked awake
the tram was stopping
hands rubbed his eyes
green and brown pulsating spots remaining in them
they fade
and slip off to the side
the metallic woman said
last stop, please exit the tram
he got out

•

Andrei closed the door to Kryštof's apartment. He hadn't been here. A spacious three-room apartment. Unfurnished. Only a couple pieces of furniture. He'd probably just moved in. He didn't look at anything closely. He was so tired he could hardly stand. He took off his shoes and lay on the bed. He fell asleep with Kryštof's smell in his nostrils.

He had a strange dream. About a killer whose mind moved through the flooded city. Whose soul, like a curse, was exchanged among empty people. About a killer who was an aberration in this world.

The killer jumped up and ran into the shadows. Steps pursued him. The aged and ailing body could hardly meet the demands of his intentions. The inflow of oxygen suffocated the smoker's lungs. Leap up to that window and then over the wall? A poor takeoff. Bad all way around. He didn't reach the ledge and fell to the ground. He put his arm back in place. He'd dislocated it. The body screamed. He knocked over some trash cans to gain a little more time. He ran to the subway ventilation shaft. Too narrow. No way forward. He doubled over and desperately gasped for breath. Something whistled painfully in his bronchi. He almost vomited from exhaustion. He looked at the shaft again. His shoulders wouldn't fit through. The footfalls of the policeman around the corner. He looked around. He grabbed a brick lying on the ground beside the air vent. He wound up and with all the strength he could muster bashed his dislocated arm several times. Extreme pain in the torn muscle. The arm was useless now anyway. He shattered the shoulder joint. He roared in pain. He gripped his shoulder and wrenched it as close to his chest as possible. It crunched like when de-boning a chicken. The injury frantically flooded his system with chemical transmitters and the nerves screamed a warning to the brain, and the killer began to worry the body might lose consciousness. He was now able to pull himself inside. The policeman appeared from around the corner.

"Freeze! Jesus, don't climb in there!" shouted a voice in a tongue the killer didn't understand. He fell into darkness.

The closed subway station. The empty vestibule. The motionless escalators. Water dripping everywhere. Trickling from metal gears. Hundreds of little paws of water running over the faux marble tiles. Mud. The tracks were underwater. Two white eyes opened just below the water's surface. The killer climbed onto the platform. The body had blood poisoning and was at a critical stage of hypothermia. He broke into a jog, as fast as the stiff muscles would allow. He tried to block out the moaning coming from his mouth.

He walked up the metal staircase. Above the exit a sign, National Avenue. Probably the name of the station. The subway station was locked. He had to break the glass door to get out. People outside began to gather, no doubt startled by his appearance. Blood was dripping from his hideous open wound onto the spit-covered pavement. Someone called an ambulance. There were several homeless people around. Without a moment's thought he walked over to one of them sitting by himself against the glass wall.

"Fuck off!" said the man's drunken voice. He wasn't as old as he looked. He was plastered, but otherwise seemed reasonably healthy. The killer fell into his arms.

The killer shoved off the old man's wet body and wiped off the blood that had dripped onto his clothing from the man's gaping shoulder. He reached into a pocket and took a soggy photo with writing on the back: *Marián Rotko*. He unzipped the jacket, took from the inner breast pocket several other photos and a folded piece of paper covered with some info. He hurriedly glanced at the paper. Part was in English, part in German, and he also recognized some Japanese symbols. He got to his feet unsteadily and stuffed everything into a pants pocket.

"Hey, that guy's robbing him!" yelled one of the bystanders.

"The police are on their way, shithead. Stop! Don't fucking go anywhere!"

He left. No one stopped him.

The killer walked toward the nonfunctioning part of the city. Toward the river. He was drunk. He needed time to sober up a bit. Not completely, because this body was already so heavily addicted to alcohol that withdrawal symptoms might create even more complications. No streetlights shined in the flooded part of the city. The reek of fish was pervasive.

He entered one of the evacuated houses and lay down on a bed soaked with river water. Everything in this part of the city had a single odor. The odor of the river. He fell into a deep sleep.

The next day he moved to another body. He was fed up with the constant need to soothe the previous one with the cheap vodka found in the body's dirty coat pocket when he awoke. A fourteen-year-old blind boy passed him downtown. The killer was kneeling on the cobblestones of Wenceslas Square acting like a beggar when the white cane came stammering by. He needed to distinguish the voice he'd heard over the telephone three days earlier. The voice alone could now lead him to the whereabouts of the local St. Petersburg connection. He needed the blind boy's hearing. He rose and seized the boy's hand. He pressed into it the photos and folded paper from the back pants pocket.

The killer shoved away the beggar and his booze stench. He put away the photos and paper. They were useless to him now. He couldn't see. All essential information about the person he was now to track down was in his memory. With the cane he explored the sidewalk before him. Finally, a healthy body. The brain functioned brilliantly, with the exception of significant dysfunction in some neural connections, which occasionally caused him to be flooded with feelings of anxiety and hopelessness (though not a particular hindrance). His hearing was perfect.

With this body he killed the local connection. He had to lie low for a while because several people had seen him do it. He hid out on a river island in the middle of the city. The floods had created an ideal environment for this purpose. No one looked for him there. He fell asleep blind with open eyes on the metal walkway of some locks for boats.

His life is now darkness and silence
his life quivers
like the distance between two stars

Long ago he learned to detach his body
to shed superfluous matter
to become merely a principle
the principle of a killer
the code of revenge
a curse
a virus
now he only thinks
he is clean and perfect
he is a singular aberration
in a safe world

He came without anyone noticing

he is everywhere in the city
he waits in the bodies of paupers
in desolate bodies destroyed by alcohol
slowly he walks the streets
in churches he drinks from the baptismal fonts
he kneels hunched on the hard cobbles in the city's center
his palms forming a bowl in front of him
and he waits
he recognizes his man by the soles of his shoes
he quietly rises and walks after him

When he killed the next one
he no longer needed a weapon
his hand easily slipped through the skin of the throat
and through that small hole
he uprooted the entire body
pulling out the root of arteries
like a massive white weed from the soil
that had grown too long

He only enters the empty ones
into those who have stopped hoping
into forsaken frames
into bodies with souls devoured by demons
into those bodies no longer actually alive
but whose cells continue mechanically to divide

He occupies the territory of the desperate

●

When Andrei woke up it was almost dark. A bird wistfully warbled somewhere outside. It sang like a dog with a smashed leg. He looked around, confused for a moment. He had forgotten where he was. He kept waking up in different places. In different cities, trains, apartments. It sometimes seemed he didn't wake up where he'd fallen asleep.

He stood at the window. Outside it reeked of wet sidewalks and streets. The sky was clear and enormous. Arching from horizon to horizon. Lamps, power lines, and crooked antennas on roofs were transformed into a network of black lines against the sky. Everything was preternaturally alive. Everything was sensed. A plethora of washed smells in the cool evening air. Grass grew in rain gutters and in cracks in plaster. Bricks were the color of dirt and confused weeds attempted to take root in them everywhere they could.

On a line in the yard damp forgotten laundry hung motionlessly. The husband of the woman who left it would walk around the whole next day in dried rainwater. In the building opposite, from the ground floor to the top floor, a column of light rose up as someone pressed the light switch in the hallway. Televisions flickered blue in apartments. For a week the only news coming from them was of the floods. The nation had had enough of endlessly staring at water. Finally the programming returned to the way it should be. The entire republic was now enthusiastically watching the latest episode of the popular American series *Empty Your Head*.

Smoke from cigarettes surreptitiously passed between children in the courtyard floated into the room. Andrei watched the cautious movement below him. The movement of the whites of a young Gypsy's eyes under the infinite evening sky.

He shut the window. The room was suddenly quiet and sad. He walked around the empty apartment of a person who had made love to his wife. He opened the cupboards and drawers and touched the clothing of someone he didn't know anymore. He expected the door to squeak open any second, and then they'd finally be face to face. He was tense all over. He wanted to face him. Look him right in the eye. He had to see him in the flesh, not through the electric signals of a telephone, not through another's mouth. He had to see him for real because this person had lost all contour for him. His form had evaporated into an ungraspable, painful, vague impression that popped into his mind every time Kryštof's name was uttered. But the door remained silent. No one came.

He started to get hungry. How long had it been since he'd eaten? He went to the kitchen. The refrigerator was empty. In the freezer he found soup, or something very much resembling soup, frozen hard as a rock. He lit a match. He let it burn in his hand a while. He embraced the ball of warmth radiating from it. As he brought it nearer, the stove ignited mutedly. A blue flower of gas bloomed. It was hot and aromatic.

As he was looking through the drawers for a spoon, to his slight surprise he came across a handgun amid the spatulas and ladles. In another drawer there was a full magazine. He took both of them. He checked if there was a cartridge already in the chamber, and when he found it empty, he stuck the pistol in the back waistband of his pants and pulled his sweatshirt over it. He slipped the magazine into his pocket. He sat down and sipped the hot soup. The spoon kept catching on a black spot where the enamel had chipped off. He put the envelope Marián had given him on the table. He waited. The apartment was completely silent, save a crumpled plastic bag quietly straightening itself out on the kitchen counter.

Meter-long raindrops fell from a great height above the city. Now far apart from each other. Made heavy by gravity, the water sometimes disturbed a black puddle that undulated the reflection of the first lights turned on in apartments.

He went outside. He was thinking about the dream he'd had. He walked toward the river. He blinked, and a string of lamps lit up in procession from one end of the street to the other. They ignited, their dim orange glow slowly gaining in strength, as if slowly inhaling. On the other side of the street a boy with a face like a greyhound embraced a girl, and as he kissed her a strand of her wet hair slipped between his lips and he drank rainwater from it. Andrei laughed to himself. He could taste it in his own mouth. At a distance of fifteen meters he could smell the same wet aroma the boy smelled. The entire world again took on impeccable clarity for him. All his senses intensified with the setting of the sun. He walked on in thought, and because the girl wrapped in the grey-hound-boy's arms reminded him of Nina, he stopped around the corner and took in their scent.

He quickly constructed from their odors a rather pleasing story. He knew they'd traveled by tram because from their palms he could smell the iron handrail they'd held along the way. They'd been somewhere out of town. The outskirts. Beyond the last houses. Their clothing was still suffused with a fresh air uncharacteristic of the city. They smelled like autumn. They were returning from a deserted park or garden where fruit trees grew. Where the wind had already begun quickly plucking the leaves from the branches and placing them on the ground, making a bed in the grass for heavy autumnal creatures to lie on silently beneath a tree on rainy nights and imbue the leaves with decay. And he smelled all the aromas of lovemaking emanating from them. He smelled every passionate caress of skin under their clothing. And these caresses enabled him to visualize the whole situation almost exactly. He saw how they slowly undressed in the leaves and how the cool earth gave them goosebumps. He saw them entwined, and how he held her wet hair in his fist, and she bit into his skin as they penetrated and passed through each other and lost themselves in bloody scratches, bruises, and the whole infinite, sweet abyss of their bodies. He saw them quietly sigh as they collapsed into the slippery leaves, covering themselves with them and falling asleep in exhaustion. Andrei yearned for the warmth of a woman's body.

He brought himself back and kept walking. He tried to remember which Prague island had locks where boats floated through. He ducked under the red-and-white-striped tape separating the flooded zone of the city from the unscathed one.

•

One hundred inhalations and exhalations
are enough for me to
track down and kill anything
there are only two things
heartbeat and breath
I measure my body's time by movements of air
a moment it belongs to me and a moment to the night sky
to leaves, the river, dirt
fur or feathers
to anything

I now run on breath alone
I exchange it with everything around me
only through it am I connected to this world
two threads of air from the nostrils

Two filaments branching out in my circulatory system

running all the way to the tiniest venules at the tips of my toes
each of my cells is fed scents from outside by them
each cell harbors a piece of the environment
lying just beyond the borders of my being

My silent lungs filled with the odor of night
my gleaming violet kidneys
the slick whips of my veins
all my bloodiness
everything inside
is in motion, contracting and relaxing
a constant flow of blood nourishing the body
distributing through it black city air

My perfect body
that perfectly fits the darkness

Andrei repeated this like a prayer as he entered the flooded area.
Beyond the border. In the low districts. The streetlights were out,
the entire area still without electricity, and his eyes were adapting
to the absence of light diluted in the sheen of street surfaces. Now
there were only car wheels in the distance occasionally splashing a
puddle onto the sidewalk. From where he stood it sounded like a
band-aid being ripped off. Like long exhalations at a window on
cold rainy days.

He descended to the river. To the inundated part of the city.
Everything was different here. Everything was marked by the
weight of the flood waves, everything was transformed and mixed
together. He created maps of those locations before his eyes. Maps
of all the new streets and lanes, passages into houses opened by
water, pathways leading through rooms where the occupants had

drowned (and for the first time their bodies saw what the neighbor's apartment looked like when a powerful current squeezed them through a crevice in the wall, demarcating another stretch of the urban riverbed), maps seeping into his mind, maps composed of pools of water, maps resembling the letters of the Japanese alphabet, resembling a haiku about fish, about the entrails of whitefish, written with a single symbol.

In the dark it took one hundred inhalations and exhalations for Andrei to distinguish the animate from the inanimate. Then he watched every movement. Hungry eyes closed and opened again in a different place. A child was born on a collapsed roof. Greyhounds caterwauled in heat there. They yowled and produced kittens.

In full stride, staying aware of his surroundings, with perfect efficiency of movement, he pulled out the concealed pistol from under his gray jacket (borrowed from Kryštof's apartment) and inserted the magazine. He racked the slide. The moment he cocked the trigger and the first round clicked in the metal chamber, a star in the sky above him silently fell. He made a wish.

The Milky Way soured. The whole universe was silent. It wrapped Andrei in a gentle breeze as he made his way.

He's on the riverbank. Standing by the now reviled water. It's swept away folks' dirty, shabby homes, and with them their lives. They hate the river and they hate each other. They washed themselves away long ago by a current far more massive and dark. He's alone here, and the river water is placid. It's everywhere. Not a single thing left unmarked. It's on the surface and clings to interiors. In cavities.

Andrei heads to the island. He tries to visualize its exact location, it should be somewhere close. It's called Children's Island as it has a soccer field, a few concrete ping-pong tables, and assorted jungle gyms, slides, and swings. On summer evenings their iron squeaks without rest into the rustle of the trees and sluice gates. Children dirty and screaming indefatigably in motion.

Now it all lies in the current. The orb of metal pipes now filters the current. Grass, branches, and a wet dog swollen with river hang from it. The children have fallen ill along with their playground. They sleep and have dreams demented by fever.

Between the island's edge and this riverbank is a system of locks — huge, metal, malevolent looking gates. One feels threatened in their presence. Probably because of the water they hold back at differing levels. Boats float through here because the weir dividing the river at the lower end of the island is unnavigable.

He walks across the stone footbridge. Though not large, the island is long. The chestnut trees that grow here are still alive despite having been ravaged by the flood, small milk-green hedge-hogs being birthed in their branches. Andrei walks along the bank. He lights a cigarette and looks a while at the moon overflowing onto the river's surface.

Then he saw him. He was sleeping at the lower sluice gates. Water poured over the flowers of rust on its walls. He pushed him to the ground with the pistol. The killer peered at him through eyes without pupils. Andrei froze . . . They motionlessly watched each other a moment. The killer gingerly touched Andrei's hand, and, almost maternally, gently stroked his knuckles.

"So we finally meet, Mr. Crow . . ." he said and forced the finger frozen on the trigger.

The shot thrust night through the boy's slim body. A trickle of blood ran from his mouth. Andrei's knees buckled. He was paralyzed by what he'd done. He felt a heat flowing into him. Fear swallowed him. He desperately tried to calm himself. His thoughts collided in his head.

Everything works.

Each thing precisely fills its space.

A vacuum is unimaginable.

The eighty-two kilos of my body's molecules in this world.

My every thought, all of my electrical impulses, just chemistry and electricity.

There is no soul!!!

There's no . . .

The killer stood a second above the bleeding blind boy. In the middle of the night, in the middle of the city, on an island that clove the muscle of the river into two fibers. He waited for the barrel to cool, removed the magazine, tucked the pistol into his pants, and pulled his jacket over it. He searched the body. He took the photos and paper with the names of those who had died and those who were to die.

He stretched out into his new body. A perfect weapon constructed merely of bones, tendons, a network of veins, a tumor in the lungs, and some memories in the nervous system. He loaded this weapon with his thought. His principle.

Into the dark he walked.

•

It was probably Saturday. He'd been lying in the shower for two hours. Dawn was breaking outside. Objects changed color in the waxing light. The water denuded him. Licked him like a dog. Licked him like a dog licks a wound. Two hours curled up under a moving film, closed inside a thin husk of rusty water. The taste of iron lingered in his mouth. Everything around him was a blur.

Everything was running together. He saw more than he should. As if two additional pupils had grown in his eyes.

He had a dream. During one of those nights. He had fallen asleep on the riverbank. He had fallen asleep in a train. He had fallen asleep in a forest covered in dirt . . . How long had this been going on? He walked through a flooded city. He slept in abandoned apartments. In the evacuated zones. Such quiet there . . .

Only water slid over his face.

It closed his eyes.

It entered one corner of his lips and slipped out the other.

He didn't remember falling asleep, he didn't remember where. And he wasn't sure if he'd actually ever woken up. The days were murky. His memory was mud and water. His memory was silt.

He walked through an unknown apartment in dim light. The smell of the people who lived there still clung to everything. He found nothing to eat but milk. He observed the destroyed street out the window. He shivered with cold. He drank mist from a cow. As if the first snow were falling into the debris . . . But it wasn't falling, he just felt it somewhere inside him. He felt snowflakes swirling within him. Like inside a snow globe with an imprisoned miniature Christmas scene.

At the end of summer the river took a stroll through the city. All sorts of things were drying in the treetops. Their stories could be imagined. The river connected everything. Through the hundreds of kilometers of its insane run across the country, it collected snippets of life from the entire population. Every detail could be imagined. The story of each piece of fabric tangled in bushes that may have once been a shirt. A shirt lying for years in someone's cottage only rarely visited. It smelled like the wooden cupboard and the cheap soap placed among the clothing. And a random board rotting in the mud might've been the remains of the very same abandoned cottage. The owners were perhaps last there in winter . . . Dead weeds populated the garden. The opening door stuck on a raised floorboard, jolting its glass panes. The snow was melting. There was no place to dry soaked boots. And the only color in the countryside was rosehip.

Or it might have been completely different . . . but does it matter?

I have to get out of here . . . he'd made up his mind.

I am the city after the flood. Swollen with foreign memory. Full of stories and memories of people who mean nothing to me.

I have to get out of here. My memory is silt.

I have to . . .

THE FLOWER

Kryštof watched his touch evaporate from the imitation-leather armrest. As the water from his handprint slowly cooled and vanished. He was trying to calm down. He watched the empty train platform from the window. He breathed. It was a hot summer night. The platform smelled of iron and grease. The smell of village fences coated with used black oil, like an old shed in the corner of a garden. It seemed to Kryštof that the stench entered his lungs along with the breath of everyone just waking from bad dreams in all the different apartments in unknown parts of the city. He felt within him how they stared goggle-eyed into the darkness and quiet of their bedrooms, into empty space, into the still shadows on the walls. He tasted the sweat a nightmare had percolated through their skin. He felt their rapid childlike breathing inside him. Breath quick as a heartbeat. Then he realized it wasn't breath, but actually the heart. His heart. Kryštof was afraid. Afraid of time. He felt something happening inside him. Like an electric current running through him. A faint tingling beneath his skin, through all his tissues.

The train was already fifteen minutes delayed. With each additional minute, Kryštof imagined the slow wilting of the flower's petals, changing color as they rotted, as they began to eat themselves. He quickly dispelled the thought. And to calm himself he gingerly ran his fingers along the edge of the large cotton pad affixed just below his ribs with an adhesive bandage and wrapped with gauze several times for good measure. The wound didn't seem to be bleeding. Good. He had to move very carefully. He consciously avoided making any sudden movements. He tried not to lean too far forward. Sometimes something inside lightly stabbed or scratched him, but it didn't hurt much.

"See how well we're getting along?" Kryštof whispered almost inaudibly. His sentence could only have been read by a deaf mute who had forgotten sound and learned to compose words from reading lips.

Outside on the platform two pigeons were fighting over the end of a bread roll. Fed up with constantly watching the departures board hanging overhead as minutes were added to the delay, Kryštof momentarily turned his attention to this sad battle. Both birds were great champions. Despite being far beyond the pinnacle of their glory days, they still had plenty of fight in them. Heavyweights. Beefy super pigeons of the Prague streets. The first had a twisted stump in place of one talon (likely from not dodging an oncoming tram in time) and limped heavily. When it would occasionally lose its balance, a ruffled wing lent support while the second bird tried to take advantage by stepping on it as often as it could. The second bird was missing its left eye and had difficulty orienting itself in the scuffle. And it was obviously very old to boot, so lacking in vigor and incapable of exploiting its adversary's mistakes to the extent it should have. The winner was pigeon one. It was clear from the beginning, and that's why Kryštof had mentally bet on it: if numero eins wins, the train will leave in five minutes. Number one jumped onto the roll end and, hobbling through foamy patches of spit, black moles of trampled chewing gum, and countless cigarette butts, victoriously dragged it off under a bench with broken wooden slats in the backrest.

Once again Kryštof was forced to consider his plight. He was nervous and now genuinely afraid. Strangely, he also felt a certain excitement that seemed inappropriate given the situation, but he couldn't help it. All at once a hot wave flooded his body as if he were looking forward to something. To what, he couldn't quite figure out. Why aren't we moving yet? He asked himself for the hundredth time and was immediately calmed. Everything was going smoothly. According to plan. For now. Everything would work out, he told himself. It shouldn't be much longer.

He was sitting alone in compartment No. 9. The second train car. Over the long years the dull light inside the train must have burned itself into all the surfaces. The whole compartment was an odd yellow. The light itself was somehow sickly. Kryštof sniffed the palms of his hands. He could smell in them every aluminum door handle, knob, and latch he'd had to grasp on the way here.

The feeble hum of electricity carried in from the outside and amplified the silence. Only the occasional movement inside the train. An enormous rusty crankshaft rotated hollowly under the floor. At least that's what Kryštof imagined when he heard the sound. Then quiet again. The soft buzz of the lamps lighting the platform . . . He ran his gaze over the rows of lights full of dead insects.

Jesus, why isn't the train moving? If only he would hear the sound of the motor starting . . . If only that delightful electric ignition would finally shoot through the train! Saint Christopher, patron of all wayfarers and my beloved namesake, please command these railway fuckers to start up the engine . . . He perked up his ears for a moment and motionlessly listened and counted the seconds . . .

Now . . .

Now . . .

Now, now, now, now . . .

Bastards . . . He furiously pounded the armrest until his fist hurt. His knuckles cracked. Annoyed, he massaged his hand. No, just no. Nothing will make them start it! They're waiting for all the passengers (and I might be the only one) to have a heart attack from this endless delay so that the train will be canceled and the conductor and engineer can go off to bed without a care. Fuckers. Death to Czech Rail! Death to all switchmen! Death to conductors! Death and endless suffering to train engineers! A horrible end to the professional spokespersons who let themselves be lured by filthy railway lucre into uttering these scandalously trite phrases about delays now coming from the loudspeakers outside!

Oof. I take it back.

Ladies and gentlemen, I apologize, of course, you're naturally only doing your jobs. Please continue to do so with love and dedication, especially now, tonight, right at this crucial moment, I implore you, unite all of your train brains and hearts, no matter the cost, after all, you have always managed together so many times before, have the master switchman put out his well-deserved cigarette and switch us over to the proper track, have sir trainmasterhighconductor set aside the porno mag he's been killing time with and start the engine, have the dispatcher, for the one-millionninehundredthousandeighthundredfiftyfifth time, with his baton, his scepter, execute that brilliant motion for which he's paid so he can support his ten-member family, and, united in glorious and admirable common effort, get this FUCKING TRAIN MOVING!!!

Nothing.

Nothing.

Nothing.

How long can they delay an international express? And for what goddamned reason? He swallowed. Calm down, he repeated to himself. Just calm down. We're waiting for another train. Trains always run late. The sun comes up in the morning, trains don't run on time. Everything is as it should be. According to plan. It won't be more than twenty minutes. Besides, I won the bet on those stupid pigeons. These things have always worked out. This is silly. Nothing to be afraid of. A few extra minutes won't matter anyway. I have enough time. Nothing to be afraid of. He almost believed it for a moment.

Nothing to be afraid of.

He leaned back. Just calm down. He took a deep breath and exhaled it long and slowly. Calm. He closed his eyes and immediately realized how painfully he wanted to sleep. The lack of sleep the past three days now fully weighed on him. He let that sweet sensation wash over him. He was deceiving his body, balancing on a thin living thread, one of his taut nerves. He knew he wouldn't allow his senses, already permeating other worlds, already touching the inchoate stuff of dreams, to tip over into the depths, into the mycelia of his life. For a moment he thought he could see the cells in his eyelids. Each of them contained a bit of light from the train platform.

The sound of steps disturbed him. Soft, almost inaudible steps that paused before the sliding glass door of his compartment. When he opened his eyes, no one was there. No one was standing outside his compartment. Kryštof again became anxious. He hadn't heard the steps continue. He stood up, carefully opened the door a little, and cast a glance down the corridor. It was empty. To the left and right. Nothing. Damn it. Nothing.

"What the hell was that?" Kryštof asked himself several times after sitting back down. His mind was racing. Could someone have noticed something not right about him? Could someone really be following him? But he'd been so careful. He mentally retraced his steps to the main train station.

•

He repeated the few words he'd said with downcast eyes to the woman behind the glass when he was buying his ticket. It's true, she did eye him with some scrutiny. He'd tried to smile, but produced more of a twisted grimace. His fingers drummed on his thigh as he nervously watched her bony fingers clatter over the computer keyboard.

"Wrocław — Main Station?" She raised her eyebrows inquisitively and looked at him as if she'd caught him red-handed doing something nefarious.

He quickly nodded his head. Another distorted smile played on his lips.

"Thanks, bye . . ." he snatched up the ticket she slid under the glass partition and quickly left. So that's how it goes. Like that. Trains. Trains. Yeah, yeah, yeah. Arrivals. Departures. That's the one. He went in that direction.

He held his breath passing a pair of police officers, one of them looked over at him, but that didn't have to mean anything. It meant nothing. The platform number for his train still hadn't popped up on the departures board. He sat on a metal bench and waited. He had time enough. He occasionally raised his eyes to the timetable to see if anything had changed. He listened to the beating of pigeon wings somewhere high up by the ceiling and continually observed the movement of people around him. He tried to remain alert yet appear nonchalant at the same time. He was so tired that he had no problem achieving the latter with perfection. The pigeon sounds were lulling him to sleep. The incessant cooing was inseparable from Prague's Main Station. People had become so inured to the sound that if it had abruptly stopped, the sudden nakedness of the other sounds would likely startle everyone.

This reminded him of something else. He'd always loved the moment when a car racing down the highway in a downpour suddenly drives under a bridge, momentarily interrupting the furious drumming of water on the car's body. It also reminded him of breaking up with a girlfriend, or when someone dies, the silence, and all those things that then become palpable as a result, all those everyday minutiae whose sudden absence hurts.

While he was considering how one becomes aware of some sounds only when they stop, how some things are understood only when they're lost, he glimpsed a swift movement out of the corner of his eye. It startled him. He nearly jumped up. He looked around in confusion. It was just one of the birds. It had glided toward him through the air and onto the tiled ground. Folks on neighboring benches smiled in amusement. Kryštof shook his head as if to say "Jesus, that sure made me jump, ha ha," but his heart pounded hard inside him for several minutes more. He was now quite awake. Meanwhile, the timetable was showing a number four for his train, so he stood up, threw his light backpack over his shoulder, and walked to his platform.

Inside the delayed Prague–Wrocław express, Kryštof wondered if he'd done something to give himself away. And to whom? The whole day he'd been paying close attention to whether anyone lurking near him had slanted eyes. The person following him logically had to be Japanese. He'd nearly lost his mind when walking through the center of town earlier that day. Never had he hated tourists so much. The Asiatic hordes of chittering photographers and videographers hungrily documenting every stone of ancient Prague had driven him to an absolute panic. He was constantly seeing someone in the crowds of tourists taking photos of him rather than of the charming towers, archways, and other nonsense. He had the feeling that one little man was suspiciously popping up in different tourist groups. When he spotted him for a third time, Kryštof panicked and, in an unguarded moment when the little bastard wasn't looking, ducked quick as a flash into the passageway of a building he was just walking past. He then spent a tense half hour peeking out from his hideout as he waited for the group to finish taking pictures of some idiot's family home.

Fortunately, he didn't notice any suspicious Asians at the train station. That was vitally important. It gave him a fragile sense of security, but security nonetheless. It's stupid to be afraid, he told himself. He laughed silently. And, to his surprise, he found that the engine had started up. Absolutely magnificent. Thank you, God. Shortly thereafter the train ponderously lurched forward on its way. Kryštof was pleased to see the increasing speed of the lights on the platform. He lit a cigarette.

The train slipped into the darkness. It was half past midnight. And it seemed completely inconceivable that someone would know the passenger in compartment No. 9 had sewn into the left side of his abdomen, under his skin, the last fertile flower of the rarest plant in this world.

•

The train glided smoothly through the sleeping city. The regular clanging of metal wheels blended with the rhythm of two hearts in two bodies. Moths slid across the windows, tiny plankton of the night. The train was hauling a load of rancid light. Individual compartments looked like empty aquariums filled with putrid water. Empty but for two, each on separate ends of the train. At one end sat an animal, a human, with a flower growing inside him. On the other, a demon, a killer concealed in a man's body.

The breath of the railroad became the breath of the only two passengers in the middle of the night. Two travelers separated by fifty meters of iron. By eight empty train cars.

Railroad breath. The raspy whisper of the rails. That long undulation. The sound of a steel band bending. Oscillating iron ribbons. The same hiss heard at rural stations by folks waiting for a train — they can't see it yet, it's around the bend, but that peculiar sound relayed through each section of track has already reached them.

It's the secret language of metal. A language spoken by things and machines. Together they agree on when to attack a person. So, a circular saw might sometimes whisper that it'll bite into the next log so badly that the hand of the man tirelessly feeding it will fall off onto its sun. Rails hiss so beautifully to lure children into the chasm of the tracks. They imitate the placid sound produced by mother's milk as it gurgles from the breast past soft toothless gums and into a hungry mouth. A scythe under a sharpening stone sings of the tenderness of a calf muscle. It could slice through it as easily as it does grass. And so on.

Even humans sometimes unconsciously use this secret language. Children understand it best. They use it to communicate through several floors of a building simply by striking a radiator. Scaffolding pipes act as interpreters between two tongues. Say anything in a human language into one end, or just slap your palm against the opening, and the other end emits a hollow, sibilant translation. A secret message to an inanimate world.

The train glides smoothly through the sleeping city. The clanging of its metal wheels sound as if underwater. Pulses of sonar. Screeching and scraping under the enormous pressure outside.

Whale songs. The hiss and swish of a massive school of sardines bursting like fireworks into a multiplicity of patterns and shapes.

Only two passengers, pervaded by the speech of iron, a conversation between wheels and rails, two passengers submersed in dull light heavy as water, on opposite ends of a train sinking into the abyss of night.

The city emits no sound. It's as silent as the Mariana Trench. As if a holy site of the sea. It seems almost impossible for someone to live in it. The station buildings and aged railcars in autumn colors, like a plowed field, with corals and seaweed slowly growing around them. Fish created by the devil settle in crevices. Fish parodying human embryos. Fish definitely not in the image of the Messiah. Fanged neon nightmares. Phosphorescent flashes in the dark. Translucent, silent beings.

Out the window it's snowing plankton. A fine pollen shaken from the wings of nightmarish moths sticks to the glass, filtered through the massive gills of the locomotive.

The train blazes an ever deeper trail. Steadily lower and lower into the darkness. Until it reaches the deepest place on Earth. The Leviathan's lair. Eyes as large as Saturn's moons. Breath that moves the Gulf Stream. Silence. The birthplace of silence. A place simulating an age before the creation of the world. A place simulating a void.

•

It was half past midnight and Kryštof was happy to notice the train picking up speed. How, at that speed, the rails running alongside the barreling train converged and connected. They slowly left behind the endless train yard sprawling out from Prague's Main Station. Blue and red switch signal lights shone into the darkness.

Sometimes a pylon of power lines popped into view behind the window. The lights of the city flashed intermittently in the gaps between the cars of decommissioned freight trains.

He was thinking.

Remembering Amsterdam.

Night.

The airport terminal. Tired travelers sitting around on metal seats. A man's head relentlessly falling and again thrusting back into an upright position in the fluid exchange between wakefulness and slumber. The occasional rustling of a newspaper as if someone were walking through fallen leaves. Every yawn slowing the world. Deafness behind glass. Giant machines silently maneuvering in a light drizzle. A sleepy approach on the runway. Signal lights. Rain.

Fear arose somewhere in his belly again. His flight to Prague was delayed. A second hour had passed and still nothing. He got up, scratched his face in contemplation, and looked around indecisively. He sighed. I have to check on it. I have to see it. Make sure it's all right . . .

He'd made up his mind. Over his shoulder he slung the single bag he was allowed to carry into the duty-free zone. He unsteadily headed off to the restrooms. He hadn't been able to sleep for two nights. Not on the plane, and not now. Impossible.

He had called St. Petersburg as soon as he landed (before he started the assignment, he'd received a Russian number with instructions to call if anything unusual happened). He learned that his Vienna contact had been eliminated. Something had started.

Kryštof asked, with a bit of a stammer, who, why, how was that possible, but received no answer. The man on the phone replied in heavily Russian-accented English that he should proceed according to plan. The next two points were Prague and Wrocław. He would be paid an even higher sum after completing the mission.

"The main thing is," the man said emphatically, in a tone that brooked no further objections or questions, "do not diverge from the original plan. Continue with your itinerary. Breaking off the mission now is unthinkable. I hope you understand me." A short pause. "It would not have exactly pleasant consequences for you, Mr. Warjak," he concluded in a completely calm, purely informative tone.

He called Marián. It was the last time he heard his voice.

Kryštof opened the door to one of the stalls. He carefully looked around to make sure there weren't any airport cameras. None. Great. He opened his bag and pulled out the wooden case containing an elaborately decorated bamboo flute. He'd bought it in the souvenir shop on the ground floor of his Tokyo hotel. He'd managed to transport the flower inside the flute with no problem. The roots were put into a plastic ampule with a supply of nutrient-enriched water. That should be enough for the whole journey and then some. He picked up the flute and examined it thoroughly until he felt two cracks, one on each side. He slipped two fingers into the flute and slowly peeled it along the cracks.

When he caught sight of the flower, his vision went dark. Dear God, not that . . . A feeling of faintness spread from his head through his throat, belly, groin, and thighs, until it reached his knees. It made him nauseous. This can't be true . . . The plant appeared to be dead. The flower was completely coiled up, sickly twisted, wilted. The water in the plastic reservoir was not depleted. Not a drop had been drunk. The monster.

Eat, you beast! Kryštof shouted furiously in his mind.

No . . . No, absolutely not! Under no circumstances can it be dead . . . !

It's not allowed . . .

Well, in that case . . . I'm in fact dead, too . . . aren't I . . .

Yes, yes, yes, hurraaaay! And Mr. Warjak gets three pieces of silver. (What a suspenseful moment that was, says the commentator of the event to the cheering audience.) On to the next round six feet under!

But, but . . . our champion was totally robbed . . . Well, Mr. Warjak, you really shook us up . . . Just lean here against the wall, nice and slow . . . There you go . . .

And breathe in. Gooood. Very good.

And breathe out. Exceeellent! Yes, that's how it's done. Now one more time! That's a clever boy, that's our lad. Yes, excellent, eeexcellent! And nice and slow, one more time . . .

And now everyone. Let's count! One and two and three and inhale ... And one and two and three and . . .

SHUT UP! Shut your damn mouth, you bastard! You fucking idiot . . . Be quiet! That's it! Enough! Fuck off . . . Fuck off.

Formica walls. Tiles. Everything blurred. Toilet. He flushed for the third time only so something would happen. One square meter. Fever had erased its contours. What now? Inhale. Exhale.

No! Just NO. It simply cannot be dead. Just. Finished. Everything's not lost. Just relax and take it slow. The problem is the water. Bad choice of nutrients. That's it. What was it doing when we found it?

Well . . . um . . .

I'm waiting . . .

. . .

Come on, out with it . . . !

Mmm . . . well then . . . how should I . . . it was eating a cat! It was growing out of a cat!

Yes! We'd never seen anything like it before . . . It's not nice and pretty, but that's just how it is! Do you get it now? If the flower is to survive, we need an animal! We have to plant it in something alive! Ha!

That's . . . but that's ridiculous . . .

No it isn't . . .

Yes it is! We've already checked in . . . Idiot. Not many pet shops generally in an airport. We're in Amsterdam. Schiphol, an international airport, if you haven't noticed yet, smart-ass. Air transport, customs inspections, no zoo, no pet shop, nothing! Super sterile. This is no rural train station. You won't even find a flea here. So where do you expect to get a cat? What? They won't let you back through check-in . . . And anyway, what about a cat with a plant growing out of it? Won't that be just a bit . . . suspicious? Huh? So? Now I'm waiting, loser! Talk! Spit it out!

Okay, okay, fine. I don't know . . . I don't know.

So we're still up shit creek.

Commentator: And Mr. Warjak gets another three pieces of silver . . .

GO TO HELL! (said in two voices; the commentator quits the scene in terror) . . .

Well . . . one possibility would of course be . . .

Kryštof vomited.

He slammed the door of the toilet stall. He washed his mouth out in the sink, washed his face. He bared his teeth at himself in the mirror. Alright fine. Fine. Let's do it.

He walked into the first duty-free shop. He bought two bottles of vodka, two plastic bottles of still water, and earrings. In a clothing shop he bought with little deliberation three cotton T-shirts, one sweatshirt, and a pair of shoes with a thickly padded tongue (the saleswoman asked if he wanted to try them on first, and he anxiously brushed her off by saying they weren't for him). He stuffed it all into a large plastic bag and set out for the restrooms at the opposite end of the terminal.

It was now late at night. He waited for a guy to finish washing his hands and leave. When the door closed, Kryštof looked into all the stalls to be safe. Nothing. In the last stall he put everything from the bag on the floor. He only left one bottle of vodka in the bag, and he smashed it against the floor. Really loud. Echoing off the cold tiles. He grabbed the bag full of glass shards and alcohol and locked himself inside the stall. He waited and listened.

Nothing.

Good. He had a blister pack of anti-nausea pills since he sometimes threw up when he flew. He bent the plastic and popped out four tablets into his sweaty palm. He dropped them into his mouth and swallowed. He opened the second bottle of vodka, held his breath, threw back his head, and quickly poured almost half of it down his gullet. His face contorted. He sat down and didn't dare move or open his eyes. His stomach rose up into his throat for a second, and he pushed it back down by swallowing.

It was over in a few moments. He drank a little more and waited for the alcohol to take effect.

And then it did!

Like someone was stepping on his head, kneeling on his temples. He opened his mouth and moved his jaw from side to side to release the pressure. Alcohol fumes burned in his nostrils.

Good.

He was wasted.

The room tilted onto its left side. It remained there, leaning crookedly on his head, until he shoved himself away from the wall and straightened up. Fuck. Maybe I shouldn't have hit it so hard. It started to tilt again. He grabbed the door handle. Stay still dammit.

He felt around for the bottle of water. He sat on the toilet bowl and took a big swig. For a moment he watched all the lines in the room run off to the side. He caught them with his eyes and returned them to their original positions.

That's enough, bitch! He roared at the door handle, which had begun to contort strangely.

Uh . . . (He realized he shouldn't be making so much noise.)

It was hard for him to stand up, and he started to undress.

Fortunately, the toilet stall was tight enough that he was easily able to hold its walls as he squirmed between them. They seemed to be shoving him back and forth.

You pig . . . he said to himself and shifted his weight to balance his haywire equilibrium. With his head bowed, he attempted to solve the equation for belt in trousers.

You goddamned pig . . . he said in the same tone as if he had meant to say: "Alright girls! Just hold on a second, we'll be back at it in a jiff, just as soon as I undo this belt here . . ."

His face slammed into the wall. He hadn't stuck out his hand in time. He hit his chin and immediately slammed his back against the opposite panel of formica.

He laughed through his nose. He even slightly hiccuped as his drunkenness began to amuse him.

He was naked.

He threw his clothes over the top edge of the stall. He reached for the plastic bag with the shards and vodka. His feet were sliding out from under him. Water had spilled onto the floor from the bottle he'd been drinking from and forgotten to close.

Pain in his knees. He curled up around the cold porcelain of the toilet bowl. He dropped off for a while.

The cold woke him up less than ten minutes later. He briefly tried to force his drunken mind to explain what he was doing there.

Then he remembered and became sombre. It took no small effort to raise himself up onto the bowl.

Now, ladies and gentlemen, it's time for Mr. Kryštof Warjak to try and make it through the last round of the competition and to the riches of the Russian mafia! An unprecedented challenge. We've never seen anything like it before! But the rules do not specifically prohibit it. Just the opposite!

Today (and this goes straight out to all our loyal viewers who've sent angry letters to our producers complaining about how little blood our previous episodes had), yes, today will really be something!

Ladies and gentlemen, dear walls, honorable loo, noble handle, lovely tiles, our favorite is now ready!

Let's give a big round of applaaaause for Misterrr . . . Warjaaaak! Hurray!

And now let's watch him rummage around in his plastic bag. Yes . . . he is riffling through glass and vodka . . . It seems he doesn't want to leave anything to chance and is taking his time to carefully select the most suitable, the biggest, the sharpest piece . . . The impulse to vomit is slightly complicating the situation for him, he's shaking a little, but that's how it usually is, ladies and gentlemen, esteemed toilet flush, dear pissed-soaked floor, that's how it usually is before such butchery . . . Yes indeed . . .

And it looks like . . . Yes . . . ! There it is. Dear viewers, there you have it! Warjak knew what he was doing, yes, yes . . . He has chosen a very fine shard! Very fine! By the way, who would've said at the beginning of the season that a fellow like him would be capable of such exploits . . . ? He's really worked hard on himself. I don't want to speak too soon, but his performance today . . . is going to be something! He is a virtuoso. A virtuoso! That's the right word. Spectators in the stands are abuzz like a beehive.

Everyone is aware that Warjak's never been in such fine form before . . .

And now we can watch him warm up . . . He's doing breathing exercises . . . And of course . . . Ha ha . . . I guess it wouldn't be him if he didn't have a nip before the start . . . A swig of vodka never killed anyone, has it . . . The organizers turn a blind eye. And why not . . . It's not like he's doping, right . . . ? He probably can't do without it . . .

Kryštof thrust the shard into his belly.

His face wrenched in pain. He gasped for breath. He sniveled. He gathered all his strength and pushed it inside. He cut through a piece of his body. Hot blood spurted onto his hand. He threw the shard to the floor. It tinkled and splashed in a puddle.

Someone opened the restroom door.

Fuck.

He clenched his teeth tightly. He didn't budge. Quiet. The slash of an unzipped fly. Quiet. Blood streaming from his wound. It made the same sound as weeping. A weak shudder. He looked at the floor. He watched the tendrils of blood branch out in the puddle. Streaking the clear water. Taking root in it. Blushing, the water changed color without much resistance. The puddle slowly expanded into the adjacent stall. He drew it back with his gaze. The guy finally started to urinate. Kryštof risked exhaling. Just don't puke. Just don't puke . . .

Half an hour later, the guy finished pissing. He flushed and washed his hands for an hour and a half. It occurred to Kryštof that during such a period of time the soap and hot water must have washed the meat clean off his bones. For at least another quarter of an hour he pulled out paper towels and grated his stumps with them until he had ground down every last piece of bone. He finally opened the door (probably with his teeth) and left.

As soon as the door shut, Kryštof grabbed the bottle and doused his wound with vodka to disinfect it. It burned like hell. When he finished grimacing and blubbering, he got down to business. He pulled out the flower (now more a wad of rot that with a little imagination remotely resembled a flower). He held it in his hand.

He hesitated.

Come on, wimp . . .

This is your last chance . . .

He was growing faint from blood loss. Like a chill running up his spine, it invidiously traversed his entire body out through the wound in his belly. Maybe the alcohol he'd drunk and the chemicals in the pills he'd swallowed were seeping out with the blood because he was suddenly sober. He just felt sleepy.

Do it . . .

With his thumb and forefinger he spread open the gash as wide as he could. With his other hand he pushed in the flower and pressed the wound closed again. He held the crumpled sweatshirt on the bleeding.

He waited to see what would happen.

Nothing.

. . .

Wait, one moment . . .

He breathed in and out.

Something stabbed him.

Then again. Then three more times. He felt something moving through his body. Such a strange feeling. As if a thread were being pulled through him. He screamed. It hurt. He had never felt so powerless . . .

He felt under attack, invaded by something foreign. He was

suddenly aware that his body was being violated. As if the cellular borders delimiting him from his surroundings were gone. Because of that tiny plant, whose growing movements he was horrified to detect inside him, the concept of what was him and what wasn't started to fracture. His body was merging with a completely different kind of living thing. The animal world was merging with the world of plants inside him . . .

He was aware of the plant taking root in him. The fibrils of its roots penetrated his flesh. It hurt. Horribly. The plant began taking from him what it needed. Blindly searching through him.

A cold sweat broke out all over his body. He started to cry. He felt it throughout his belly. It was working its way down his left leg. Then upward toward his heart. He leaned his head back, and as if sticking it out above the surface of water he frantically gasped for air. My God my God my God . . .

And then suddenly it stopped.

He swallowed.

He didn't dare move.

It was gone.

No.

It was in him, but it wasn't moving.

He could precisely distinguish how far it had reached.

It wasn't moving.

It wasn't moving.

. . .

It wasn't moving.

He breathed out.

He carefully got to his feet. He breathed deeply. His heart was pounding. He felt shaky. Adrenaline frothed in his head, having been discharged by his terrified body. He felt like he had cancer, or something similar. He felt awful. But it had stopped moving, that was the main thing. He pulled back the sweatshirt; he wanted to tie it around his waist. To his surprise, the wound was no longer bleeding.

Strange . . .

He opened the second bottle of water. The plastic band securing the cap cracked. He poured water all over himself. He washed off the blood. He carefully cleaned his wounded side. It truly wasn't bleeding anymore.

Great. Why not?

He took one of the T-shirts and the earrings he'd bought. He undid the shirt's stitching with his teeth. On the third try he managed to extract a long green thread. Good, good . . . He grabbed the bottle with the last of the vodka and took a slug. Warmth. Yes . . . He removed the hook from one of the earrings (in the shop he had carefully chosen ones with the thinnest and sharpest hooks). He tied the thread to the hook . . . Took another drink . . .

He stitched up the wound.

It didn't hurt any more than when the flower was threading its roots through him.

Vodka.

Onto the stitches and into himself.

He noticed it wasn't getting him at all drunk anymore. He ripped out the thick foam padded tongues from the shoes he'd bought and applied them like a swab on the wound (no longer bleeding, but just in case). He bandaged them with strips torn from the T-shirt. He wiped up the floor. He got dressed. He dumped the whole mess among the crumpled paper towels in the large waste container by the sink. He rinsed his face. He looked at himself in the mirror. He practiced the facial expressions he'd give at the last security check before boarding the plane.

Pretty good . . .

Hmm . . .

It should be OK . . . Just another drowsy (moderately sloshed) passenger. Yeah. Or maybe not . . . ? It is late . . . Right . . . ? He's had a bit to drink . . . that's clear. Here's your passport. Next . . . ! Next!

That's basically how it . . . could go . . . right?

Yeah. Probably.

●

Black window. Nothing beyond the city. The hiss of the tracks and darkness.

Kryštof thought about what he'd learned from Marián.

He was back.

Ruzyně Airport. HAVE A GREAT DAY IN PRAGUE. It was a joy to read the Czech signs. Carons and accents. The right words. Everywhere the right language! That familiar feeling of security upon returning home. The feeling of immediately being embraced by the first tongue he had known. The sun was shining. The clear afternoon light burned into his eyes. He sneezed as the tickle passed from his eyelashes into his nose. It's all behind me now . . . he told himself (although he didn't much believe it). He laughed at the sky. He took a bus to the city center. He had plenty of time.

It was a beautiful summer's day. Floods had destroyed the lower part of the city. The sun had returned after the relentless rain. The city was bustling with activity, a frenetic cleanup in full swing. The army, volunteers, and others. None of it interested him much.

He sat down in a garden pub. He urgently needed to eat something. He had three beers and a double espresso. He observed the angular shadows chestnut leaves cast in the fine breeze onto the tables transform into various geometric shapes. The city murmured pleasantly around him.

He just sat there for a long time. He allowed himself to be rocked on the calm waves of conversation from neighboring tables, the gentle clinking of glasses, barking dogs, and the bustle in adjacent streets. A tram cheerfully clanged its bell at an old lady belatedly hobbling across the street. Cars were honking that day as if just for the hell of it. No one was angry at anyone. Everyone was happy, full of hope. The result of all this surrounding harmony and joy was that Kryštof's eyelids drooped and he dozed off.

He was awakened by the waitress with a gentle hand, sweet smile, and his bill, on which he was charged an extra beer.

He paid and left.

He wanted to stop by his apartment. He hadn't been there for a long time. He hadn't even completely moved in yet. But right now that didn't matter. He needed a shower, clean clothes, bandages. Then he'd go to meet his contact at the agreed place. The Russian waited for him every night in Duplex Club on Wenceslas Square. Duplex was a disgusting discotheque where all of Prague's trash gathered.

He walked home, watching the city as he went. It seemed to have returned to the times of his childhood. Enchanted, full of hazy expectations, he observed the familiar districts, out-of-the-way lanes, and unkempt, dirty little parks on whose benches was carved the gospel of lowlifes and those who often possess only three things: hunger, a belly full of alcohol, and a cart of rusty iron. Evening was approaching. Plaster was crumbling off the walls of the old Gypsy apartment buildings. The smell of ash wafted from their courtyards. Children ran around screaming. The passageways were damp and drew the summer evening into their chill. A strange white fluff floated through the air, tiny tufts of mold, like snow without water. Kryštof squinted his eyes from them and laughed. He felt great. The sun illuminated every grain of dust in the air. He breathed all of it in.

He unlocked the door of his apartment. Nothing new. Through the window sunlight fell on the wall and floor. He slammed the door behind him and lit a cigarette. He tried to phone Marián, but he didn't pick up. Then he noticed the letter lying on the kitchen table. His address was written on it. The return address was Marián's.

How could the postman have gotten inside? Kryštof thought as he opened the envelope.

He pulled out two pieces of paper. They were covered in Marián's barely legible handwriting. It looked as if he'd been in a hurry. He had crossed out often.

Every line he read sapped Kryštof's previous joy, and he scanned the end of the letter with considerable nervousness. All of it was about the flower he now had inside him . . .

This is an extremely poisonous, ancient plant species. From what's been recorded, only one man long and secretly cultivated it somewhere in southern Japan during a period of unrest and samurai wars — the Eikyō era (1429–1441). The man was an impoverished lower daimyō, lost two sons in battle, and through the betrayal of his allies, his whole family and retinue were scattered. The society of the day shunned him as if he were a beggar, and he lived out the rest of his life in shame and misery on his crumbling estate. Desperate, he decided to invest all his remaining resources into the cultivation of the most beautiful image of sadness anyone had ever seen . . . that's how the plant was created, according to the legend.

Many stories and myths surround the flower. It was veiled in secrecy for its dark beauty. Mystery attracts. Everyone wanted to have it. And you know how the Japanese are when it comes to flowers. "Ikebana" and all that . . .

It is said that when the flower was brought to the indigent daimyō, he was absolutely mesmerized by its beauty. He had it put into a bowl of water, as if it were a water lily. But the flower wilted. He did everything in his power to save it, but nothing worked. Then one morning he found the flower dead. It had all been for nothing. He sank into deep despair. He'd squandered everything he owned on the plant . . . He secluded himself at home for three days and ordered that no one disturb him because he would be devoted to prayer. No one knew what was going on. When his servants dared to enter five days later they found their lord dead. He had committed "seppuku." And the flower, to their surprise, was alive.

The Japanese have so many myths on this subject. They call it "migawari ni tatsu" (loosely: "act like a replacement"). It was believed the gods could aid a human by transferring the soul to another being, giving it life in exchange for the human's death.

The story of the man who gave his life to a flower soon reached even the royal court, where it made a huge impression. The romance and tragedy of the whole legend had a deep impact on noble society.

It seems the flower was later planted in the home of one family from the upper echelons of Tokyo society distantly related to the daimyō, so they claimed it as their heritage. This family had a kind of monopoly on the cultivation of the plant for a long time and sold it for enormous sums to the aristocrats of the day. It was often considered so exclusive and desirable for its hallucinogenic effects that a drug was extracted from it . . . But that's not what it was really about. The most amazing thing is that the flower's a parasite! You've probably already found that out yourself. And as you also know, parasites always have interesting and ingenious plant mechanisms . . . BUT . . . This is really something special. This flower, and pay attention now, this flower is something like a link between the animal *and plant kingdoms. It's simply half-animal and half-plant. Not one or the other and somehow ingeniously performing mimicry. No. An absolutely awesome, AWESOME phenomenon . . . But back to the story . . . So, that family was doing business with the flowers. They were selling them as jewelry!!! Now brace yourself, you should probably sit down, or grab hold of something . . . The flower is a parasite on living organisms. It grows only on living things. The highest nobility voluntarily let the flower take root inside their bodies! They wore them on their faces! In other words, they allowed themselves to be invaded . . . They had them blossoming from their temples or from the skin under their ears. It was considered a sign of the highest prestige, wealth, and luxury. The epitome of decadent fashion . . . Something akin to when noble Chinese ladies would have their feet bound to the point of such distortion that they became seven-centimeter-long talons, and then they'd just lie around because they couldn't walk anymore due to the pain it caused them. The whole thing is totally unbelievable, amazing, perverse . . . Those aristocrats voluntarily became symbionts with this unreal parasite. But it wasn't without risk. If the flower was in any way damaged (breaking even a single root was enough), even the minuscule amount of poison that then oozed from the plant would kill its host. The advantage was that death wasn't at all painful, just the opposite. The person reportedly died painlessly, stupefied, flooded with the sweetest thoughts and dreams. Death of this kind may have even become a kind of fad, a one-off "amusement." A clandestine group of nihilists formed whose members showed a shocking disdain for life, and allegedly they held secret sex parties where they practiced all sorts of cruelties that often ended in mass suicide using the plant you now have . . .*

But anyway . . . The family made huge profits off this bizarre fashion, and, one day, they were cursed by a high-ranking official whose wife was inadvertently poisoned by one of their plants . . . and because the curse was uttered in a fit of desperation and indignation, with the maximum

level of rage and conviction to induce harm, no one doubted its effective-
ness. The curse essentially called for the family to be sooner or later wiped
out, scattered, annihilated. He even cursed the flower, screaming that it
was the devil's flower. It would bring death to whomever desired it . . .

This stigma has stuck with the flower since. Soon, no one wanted to
have anything to do with it. And if they did, it could only be for perverse
reasons. The family gradually lost all its influence and prestige. They
dropped lower and lower on the social ladder, until they and the flower
were forgotten for good.

The flower became a hereditary "jewel" as well as a curse hanging
over this dispirited Tokyo family. Only the minimum number of plants
necessary for preserving the species were maintained. It was said later that
the flower had gone completely extinct. The family lost its standing for
good, living as outcasts, and it was generally assumed the plant and the
family died out together.

This has now been proven wrong. I'm writing what I discovered so
that you realize what you've decided to sell. Most likely the most amazing
plant that has ever and will ever exist . . . No price can be put on it. All
the money you've gotten and will get for it is laughable . . . Its value is
absolutely somewhere else.

Kryštof crumpled up the letter and set it on fire in the ashtray. On
the flames of all that burning information, he lit another cigarette.
He inhaled the secret. He nervously paced the apartment.

What I'd really like to know now, he repeated in his mind, is
how to get the flower out of my body . . .

What?

You haven't written anything about how to remove the jewel . . .

He stopped and drummed his fingers on the kitchen counter.
Then he remembered. He opened the second drawer and rum-
maged through cutlery and wooden spoons. Nothing. He rifled

through the other drawers. Spoons, a bottle opener, stupid forks and knives. Otherwise nothing. Shit. He went through all the drawers again just to be sure . . .

It was here somewhere . . .

Letter on the table. But right here . . . I definitely left it here . . .

He dialed Marián's number again.

He listened to the ringtone and looked out the window. A tiny bird hopped among the branches of the tree growing in the yard. Maybe a sparrow. Long electric tones. He heard his own breath rasping in the receiver. The sparrow finally darted onto a branch and jerkily, robotically, scanned its surroundings.

Nothing.

He slammed down the phone.

He decided to go over there.

Marián didn't live far. Kryštof walked, but the city was by far not as pleasant as it had seemed at first. He puffed away the fluff that tickled his nose and stuck to his lips. The sun sank slowly behind the rooftops, accentuating the delicate, interwoven structure of chimneys and antennas. He was sweating. He had the feeling that all the bones in his body had grown heavier. He regretted not showering before leaving his apartment.

He eventually jumped onto a tram and took a seat. Somewhat relieved, he took in the swarming figures in the twilit streets. A grocer was throwing out shriveled carrots and bruised apples in front of his shop. In the window of a butcher shop a woman in an apron was pulling down the shutters with a hook. A dog was licking a pole it had just urinated on. Prague.

At the entrance he rang the bell labeled with Marián's name.

Nothing.

He rang several more times, no response. He stepped back from the entrance and looked up toward Marián's bedroom window. He bent down and searched the ground for a suitable rock and threw it. He heard it click against the glass.

Nothing.

He threw another just because, then turned around and left.

After sundown, he spent three hours in the club where he was supposed to meet his connection. Styepanov didn't show. He waited. He drank white rum with a squeeze from a shiny green half-moon of lime. At eleven he paid and left.

He was getting worried.

Something was wrong.

Get away as quickly as possible . . . pounded in his head. The quickest way out of Prague. He's here . . . He's definitely already here. He's taken out Styepanov . . . He's waiting for me somewhere right now. Maybe in my apartment. He was already there. I'm incredibly lucky I missed him. So that means . . . I can't go back there. So . . . yes, the train station. Wrocław.

There's still Wrocław.

He quickened his pace.

•

The train pulled away from the platform. It was half past midnight. The dirty streets of Prague outside the window sped up, illuminated by the turbid orange glow of streetlights. They sometimes passed bars, full of sleepy cab drivers, gaudy with vivid electric names or advertising above them.

Neon.

Neon has all the colors of the rainbow.

In the beginning of the city

was the word
written in light.
The first letter intermittently flickered
and went out.

In the last car on the opposite end of the train, the killer exhaled smoke. Fatigued from his fast and bloody journey from Tokyo, he sat down. He had time. His gleaming eyes reflected the light of the strange city.

He had walked through the entire train and knew exactly where to go, exactly what compartment to open and who would be sleeping there, exactly what he would find inside him. And he knew there was no hurry. It was no longer about the flower that belonged to his family, once august and influential, now ruined and in decline. He had nowhere to return to. His father had taken his own life without leaving anyone a note. When they found him, his body was smiling in the spot where the blade had entered him, happy perhaps because he'd finally found a reason to do it. He killed himself because of the flower.

Neither was it about lost honor nor about his own life. Ultimately, he had no life. His existence in this confused place, in this confused swarming of human lives, began with the uttered curse. It had set everything in motion and its fulfillment would close everything again. His revenge was intoxicating and self-sustaining. It ended in emptiness. His revenge was like breaking open the surface of water with a stone. He knew the quiet that came when the water closed again.

The killer breathed for an hour. He only partially belonged in this world. He was born to cursed parents, who had long ago inherited a flower created out of one man's bottomless grief. His DNA contained an atom of darkness. Stories circulated about his family that he didn't believe. His mother, whom he had never known because she died in childbirth, was rumored to have copulated with a demon. His father lost his mind over it. But he well knew it wasn't true. The useless talk of useless people.

During his travels he had encountered so much misery and vanity he no longer understood anything. So much bitterness and anguish. Filth and futility. He did not at all comprehend what was driving people. The desperation of mortal bodies. Frantic battles with cancer, alcohol, diabetes, with ingrate progeny, aging, boredom, loneliness, apathy, emptiness, with the whole wretched future. With each successive day flagging minds had to be forced not to think about death, not to think about anything fundamental. The singular recipe for how to survive was to dig deep into the mundane, turn on the television and believe that those famous mugs would say something redeeming, something to justify us alone . . . and they say all sorts of things . . . An unremitting carousel of bullshit.

During his travels, the killer had accumulated in him a great many memories belonging to strangers. He had no memories of his own. He remembered nothing but the curse. He'd had no childhood. As if he had never lived. He had traveled through the most blighted areas of this society. His character was gradually forged out of the despair, injustice, and nostalgia of the forsaken and the errant. The bitterness inside him was greater than any other being had ever tasted, or ever would.

It was always the same. As soon as he encountered resignation or despair, he reached for it. It was like thrusting his hand into a hive. His bare palm stroked the hot honeycombs of memory inside. That was where he would firmly take hold. The seething honey oozed through his fingers. The heat poured into his mind. That subtle quivering. The dance of bees passed through him like chills. And once again he would draw breath in another's body.

The killer recalled a series of distant events in the lives of people he didn't know. He remembered desolate places in gardens, in foggy landscapes from childhoods he'd never lived. He remembered learning how to ride a bicycle in an Ostrava housing estate, his first cigarette beneath an overpass in the middle of the pouring rain, and another first cigarette in another person's life he'd visited. He remembered making love with his first girl. Once it was in the cellar of a prefab apartment building, another time in a barn on a pile of hay, or on a couch in a tacky apartment. In this current body he now remembered someone called Nina, and also a little girl named Kristýna, who was poisoned by mushrooms, and, God knows why, he felt sorry.

This was his life. He filed through memories and past events as it pleased him at the moment. He carried inside him the stories of many people — assorted variants of time frittered away, lives crippled, and days wasted in futility. Each of these stories ended badly. They ended in him.

•

Kryštof fell asleep and dreamed.

He was in his apartment, but it looked different. He knew all the rooms and individual objects, but it was as if they weren't his. As if he didn't belong there. He was sitting in the room where he had his flowers, his personal collection. He also used to sleep there, surrounded by gorgeous poisonous flowers.

A muggy night outside. Unbearably muggy for several days running. The floodwaters had subsided, the cleanup work had begun, and a heat wave had set in. The flooded streets stank of rot and drying debris. The city was full of it. Wind carried the reek of dying river branches that had been cut off in some neighborhoods and basements when the river receded from the streets.

An overwhelming stench and mugginess outside. But it was good for the flowers. Kryštof watched as they became lush, damp, and opened new flowers. As if too fully alive. As if licking themselves within.

He noticed the skin on his hand was darker than usual. At that moment he realized it wasn't actually his body, but Marián's. And the apartment wasn't his, either, but Marián's, which was why it was so familiar to him. As if he had temporarily put on Marián's perspective. His perceptions and life. In the dream, it somehow seemed completely natural.

The air was completely still, so it surprised Kryštof when the kitchen window slammed. He stood up and looked across the room. Nothing. He hesitantly entered the kitchen and reached for the light switch. It didn't work. Damn . . . he hissed into the silent room. He flipped the switch several times. Then he noticed a light bulb lying on the table. Something started to open inside him. Something black reached out for his stomach and heart. He gulped. His hands were shaking. He then heard behind him a quiet rasping of metal being unsheathed. Kryštof turned around with a jerk.

He came to half undressed lying prone on his bed. He was tightly bound to it in several places, he almost couldn't move. It was night outside. He immediately felt pain. On the left side of his abdomen, just under the ribs. He raised his head as much as he could and screamed. His body was bathed in sweat. He was wounded. His body was open there. But this wasn't what frightened him. The wound was filled with soil, and a small plant was growing from it. A tiny, living shoot of pale green.

He let his head fall on the pillow. He bit into his lower lip. He was in agony. It was the exact same feeling he'd recently experienced.

The roots groped around his organs, extending and contracting like octopus tentacles. They crept through him like slender, needle-sharp worms.

He was under attack.

Hour upon hour he watched the flower grow.

It slowly plundered him.

The more it lived, the less strength he had. In the end he was only able to vaguely make out how it burst open and sprouted a magnificent, giant crimson flower. It all happened over one night and the following day.

It was evening. Streaks from the sinking sun crept along the walls. It must have been a glorious day out. When he heard someone repeatedly ring the doorbell, he no longer had the strength to move. Only a faint murmur escaped his lips. A sound no longer human. Suddenly, a rock clinked against the windowpane, and then another a moment later . . .

It was night again. With great effort, he raised his eyelids one last time when someone entered the room. It was a man. He focused his vision. The man reminded him of someone. Maybe someone from his childhood . . .

The man came nearer, bent down toward the flower, and touched its petals. He felt a pulse in them.

"Kryštof . . ." said Marián hurriedly, almost feverishly, "Kryštof, everything got screwed up somehow. You should know . . . You will never get the flower out of you . . . It won't let you . . . It won't let you deny it the nutrients your body is giving it now . . . Understand? It won't let go of you as long as you live. The only way to be rid of it is to die . . . Why'd we ever get mixed up in this? Why . . ." He didn't finish because a stranger's hands had taken his flower.

A terribly heavy, metal object sank through water into the cold and dark at the bottom of a lake.

•

The train left a slipstream in its wake. It opened an air hole that closed up a moment later. The bushes along the tracks moved like hair underwater. The slipstream drew them in, forcing them to stretch into emptiness. Into places that would make a person recoil. The last car seemed to be dragging an enormous weight. The still living root of the train, trying to take hold somewhere in the landscape. A root created by the train simply being a train. The smell of sleeping people, their wet breath, and the light that changed a thousand times inside the grooves scratched in the windowpanes, in a rhythm born of iron. Like an echo of a strange recording, it all hung in the air above the rails for a moment even after the last car passed. Weeds growing between the ties, without anyone noticing, had stopped subsisting on sunlight and begun to live solely on what the trains left behind.

Even the killer, leaning out the window of his compartment, swallowing wind and listening to the nocturnal landscape, felt he had inhaled something foreign, unfamiliar. The Polish border was less than half an hour away. He leisurely finished his cola, tore the bottle with his teeth, and slowly, carefully unwound a thin, half-meter-long strip of plastic. He put it in his pocket and went into the corridor.

Silent as air, like the breath of a sleeping girl, the killer walked from car to car. His steps emitted no sound. They didn't touch the floor.

•

Kryštof opened his eyes. He looked around for several seconds to orient himself. He was in the train. He confusedly lifted up his T-shirt and touched the bandage on his belly with a sweaty, trembling hand.

"So that's the deal?" he asked in terror. He clenched his teeth so hard his ears hummed. It'd been a dream. It had only been a dream. Just a dream.

He looked out the window and gradually calmed down. The train was slowing. Some bushes passed by the window. Kryštof exhaled in wonder. No, they weren't bushes. They were passing a field of hogweed. Giant Hogweed rose up in his mind. It had been such a long time since he'd seen so many of them together. But someone had actually told him it grew in dense patches at the border.

The train continued to decelerate, so he could clearly distinguish individual plants. They emerged silently from the dark. Kryštof gazed at them until they disappeared again on the other side of the window. They were monstrous. Huge, oversized, veined stems, thick as arms and full of water in their cavities. He remembered how he'd feared them as a child. He laughed. He immediately began recalling all the information he had once amassed about them. Their sap opens a pathway in the skin for sunlight. Pigment changes. Hogweed spreads like a virus, like a flaw in the landscape. It kills every living thing around it. Hogweed is an anomaly in the world of plants. It harbors something secret inside. As Kryštof now gazed at that monstrous weed, he felt an odd compulsion, a certain aversion and disgust combined with a strange desire to touch the immense cellular mass, to feel through the warm animate walls of its body the poison hidden within. A desire to rid himself of the old fear that had paralyzed his entire childhood . . .

Kryštof was torn from his thoughts by the disconcerting realization that the train was now moving at a mere footpace. A moment later it stopped entirely. It was surrounded on both sides by a field of hogweed. Some of the plants towered over the train.

Kryštof stood up and pulled down the window. An oppressive stench came from the field. He paced the compartment from door to window a few times. He smoked a cigarette. Finally, he opened the door and walked into the corridor. He stood and listened. It was dead quiet. He was all alone in the train car. Maybe even in the entire train, he thought. The air outside trembled with the sound of insects, the high voltage of a summer night. And he thought he heard water dripping somewhere. He suddenly realized the conductor hadn't come by the whole time . . .

And then he remembered that he wasn't alone on the train.

Those steps. God . . . Those steps he'd heard in the corridor when they were still in Prague. He felt the pulse in his head quicken. He tried to think. Prague, delay, steps, conductor. He froze. What was that? Somewhere at the other end of the train a door slammed. Someone had just entered his car.

Kryštof panicked.

He ran back into the compartment. He leaned out the window, into different air. Into the darkness.

He hesitated.

He glanced at his backpack. No.

He heard a strange rustling coming from the corridor . . . as if someone were dragging fabric along the floor . . .

He climbed out the window. He hung by its edge. He looked down over his shoulder. Less than a meter. He let go.

When he hit the ground the left side of his belly throbbed in pain. In the place where the flower was hidden.

Dammit . . . he hissed. He grabbed his side. It left blood on his hand. He turned around, and after a brief deliberation, slipped in among the hogweed.

Cautiously, so as not to break even the smallest branch or leaf, he wormed his way in among their stalks. He could clearly distinguish the large green ducts inside them. He felt foreign substances on his mucous membranes. A dead, decomposing, vegetal humus was smeared out under his feet. Sweat stung his eyes, and his head was spinning.

Is this a kind of plant fever or what? he thought in disgust.

When he had crossed the border where the light ended, he paused and slowly, ever so slowly, turned around. He attentively observed the train. He wiped the sweat from his face and tried not to notice the stench of the rotting vegetation under his feet. Something was moving down the corridor. A shadow was slowly walking through the car. Kryštof tensely watched its movement wide-eyed.

The demon stopped in front of his compartment. He went inside and looked out the window for a time. Then he silently swung himself into the darkness, slipping from the window like water. He landed in a crouching position and remained like that without moving. Kryštof knew he was looking right at him. The man's eyes appeared to have no irises, only whites.

What the?

"Andrei . . ." sounded hoarsely through Kryštof's dry lips.

His vision blurred. He couldn't focus.

That's impossible . . .

"Andrei?" repeated Kryštof, this time sounding more like a cough.

"Andrei . . ." he whispered deliriously. "Andrei, help me . . ."

"Help me!" he exhaled with great effort.

Kryštof wanted to get back on the train, but it was impossible. He wearily crouched on the ground. Not out of fear, but necessity. The whole world was swaying beneath him. He could hear insects rubbing their legs together. The sound of crickets slowed. It acquired a completely new frequency, adjusted to the movement of blood in his body. He saw the poisonous sap phosphorescently shining through the massive stems of hogweed pulsate at the same tempo. He was breathing air directly from the soil. Something exploded in his veins. He got stuck in the infinite space between two beats of his own heart. He heard each wet reverberation, the opening and closing of his valves, separating his heart's ventricles and atria. He heard their beating as plainly as if someone were vigorously smacking their palms against a raw side of meat right by his ear. He was caught in the infinity of a single systole and diastole. In a single desperate twitch of the heart that, trapped and suffocating in his rib cage like a fish in a net, seemed to be convulsively trying to tear itself out of his body.

For ages his gaze held the gaze of the demon with the face of his friend in a field of hogweed. The train started to move again in the rhythm of Kryštof's body, in the rhythm of the poison in vegetal veins, in the strokes of cricket legs.

The killer swung himself back into the train in an endlessly long movement. The train seemed to slowly inhale him. Kryštof curled up around a stalk of hogweed and fell asleep.

•

The train had stopped. The killer entered the compartment and looked out the open window into the darkness amid the huge plants. He could easily make out his victim's thermal image. He jumped out and waited. He sensed the hatred coming from those mammoth organisms rising up before him. He didn't know why, but he was sure he wouldn't make it through their barrier without being mangled by them. Several turned their broad crowns to face him. They must have sensed in their midst that sublime flower decaying and dying in the body of a man. They wouldn't let the killer through to him.

But the killer knew something more than the man with the clearly outlined heat signature gleaming in the dark and commanding his attention. The killer saw the thermal borders of his every organ. Every individual vein. And among all that living, pulsating matter, he saw a cold spot from which death radiated in all directions like a star. A place just under the skin where the broken flower was concealed as it slowly, like a wounded animal, curled into itself. And he saw the poison seep into the man's circulatory system.

The train slowly started. The killer leaped back inside. He still had one more meeting in Wrocław.

The night sky was clear. The raw glare of stars accentuated the lines of track. It accentuated the metal and glass of the train as it almost noiselessly picked up speed. It accentuated the embryo protected by the branches of giant plants.

•

They were already waiting for him in Wrocław. Two Ukrainian butchers had been sent to assist the lone Bardyaev. Assassins without conscience or memory. The meeting point was in a decrepit abandoned factory on the edge of town. It was cold and damp. Low clouds, dirty and rent, flitted through the chill sky. The tops of trees rustled darkly and erratically, creaking in their roots. A rather grim day.

As soon as he arrived at the meeting point, a shot tore off a piece of his flesh above the collarbone. The pain exploded in him like ink in water. He dove behind a half-demolished wall and pulled out the pistol with his good hand. He slid in the magazine. Bullets whizzed past his head, bit off pieces of brick and whirled up dust. He bandaged his shoulder with his torn shirt, clenching one end of the fabric in his teeth.

Metallic taste.

He choked off the blood.

They held each other in check for eight hours. One of the goons tried to get at him from the side. He shot the kidneys out of his body. Then he listened to his death in the middle of the hall for three hours. It sounded as if he were being born again.

A rain shower in early evening gave way to a clear sky by dusk. A beautiful sunset. Night. No one was in a hurry. The killer drank from the milk among the stars. He was suffering blood loss. He'd also run out of ammunition. Now he was loaded just with breath.

When only Bardyaev remained, the killer reached into his own body and removed the bloody tumor from inside his lungs. He loaded it and stood up. He zigzagged across the space of the hall. Bardyaev had one last bullet, and missed. The killer shot him with cancer.

Bardyaev's knees buckled. He started to cough. He barely had two days to live.

When he raised his eyes, the killer was no longer there.

•

Andrei woke from a long dream, curled up on a park bench. He sat up, confused. He was extremely weak. His first movements told him something was wrong. He apprehensively touched his shoulder wrapped in the bloodstained shred of his shirt. It hurt. A lot. People walked by and pretended not to see him, or stole a glance at him in disgust. He guessed he probably didn't look so hot. Blood was caked on his arm. Also on his clothes. He was a mess. His hair was wet. It'd probably rained, he thought . . .

He found some photos in a pocket. He examined them carefully. Two unknown people . . . And Marián . . . he raised his eyebrows in surprise. His name was even written on the back of the photo . . . *Marián Rotko.*

Aside from the photos, he had two folded pieces of paper in his pocket. The first, quite worn and crumpled, had writing in English that appeared to be a series of personal info: telephone numbers, addresses, names. Some of the names were crossed out. Much of the info had been added to in a different handwriting, even in different languages. He recognized the German. Then some symbols that looked like Japanese . . . He casually skimmed the text, not understanding even one of the languages. But suddenly something caught his eye. In one line he clearly recognized three words: Warjak, Prague, Wrocław.

The other paper contained a short list. A quick and simple summary. He was startled because the handwriting looked just like his. It truly seemed he had written it himself . . .

The hand holding the paper trembled as he read:

Khalkin – dead

Styepanov – dead

Bardyaev – dead

Rotko – dead

Warjak – dead

Warjak – dead, he read again quickly . . . Rotko – dead . . . What on earth was going on?

He understood none of it . . .

What did it mean . . . dead?

Warjak – dead . . . he reread it one last time . . . He turned the paper over. Maybe just to see if there was something that might explain it, but apart from a few smudges of dried blood, there was nothing. He crumpled up the list and threw it in the trash.

Why?

Why did I write that?

When?

He abruptly stood up. He looked around in confusion to make sure no one was watching, but then he realized it hardly mattered. It was cold. He dug his hands deep into his pockets and quickly distanced himself from where he'd woken up. He looked back a few times. He felt like he'd done something bad, he just didn't know what. He walked off in a random direction through the park and away.

He entered the foreign city. The people he passed seemed not to see him at all. Someone walking past painfully slammed a shoulder into him and didn't even look back, no apology, nothing. It even seemed people were walking through him. Like he was just air. Everyone was overtly ignoring him. Or maybe . . . they really didn't see him . . . Am I dead? he thought. He looked at his hands for a sign of his own death, but found nothing . . . He was finally calmed by an old lady scornfully eyeing him with a scowl. At the moment she realized he was watching her, too, she turned away and waited patiently with a plastic bag in hand while her dog finished defecating on the sidewalk. Andrei was so grateful for this moment proving his earthly existence that he didn't even say anything vulgar to the woman, which he would have done in ordinary circumstances.

He noticed everyone was speaking strangely. He couldn't properly understand anything they said . . . It only dawned on him a while later that the snippets of language he caught from passersby were in Polish.

He came to a train station. The building was monumental, with high windows, a turret on each side, and battlements on the roof reminiscent of a castle, on top of which were the dark yellow neon letters: **WROCŁAW GŁÓWNY.**

He shook his head in disbelief.

•

Andrei bent down and picked an apple out of the grass. It had already started to rot, covered in concentric white rings of mold. He threw it into the wheelbarrow with the others. It banged against the tin. From under three massive trees he raked the rest of the browning leaves into a pile while picking out several forgotten walnuts encased in slimy black husks. He wiped them off and put them in his pocket. He lit a match and set the leaves on fire. The smoke stung gently inside his nose . . .

All at once it occurred to him that he'd already experienced this situation. All of this had happened sometime before, but try as he might, he wasn't able to recall when. He stood and breathed the smoke pouring out over the garden like milk strained through the planks in the fence and into the fields. The moment stretched out like a string of honey. All the rhythms in his body coalesced. Everything slowed.

Andrei felt his heart pounding. He laughed. The world had made sense again for a while now. They'd left the old house. Left the country where their daughter had died. They had started over, from the very beginning. They refused to speak about anything that had happened before . . . In one simple stroke, they had crossed out their past life and directed their attention to the future one. They'd had nothing left to lose . . .

His eyes scanned his surroundings. They had it pretty good here . . . They'd gotten used to it in the two years since they'd moved. He'd found work at a fish factory in Gdansk. He wasn't making a fortune, but it was enough. And he truly could not imagine a more beautiful place to live. It was less than an hour's walk from the village to a beach that was covered in snow in winter and rainy in summer, but when it was nice out you could walk along it for fifty kilometers in either direction without seeing another soul.

Andrei bit his lower lip, tilted back his head, and sent a thought skyward.

At that exact moment, Nina was holding her breath, submersed in the lukewarm water of the bathtub. Through the open bathroom window the aroma of burning leaves entered with the rays of the autumn sun and the clang of garden tools as Andrei put them away in the shed. She listened to the clamor for a while underwater, then reemerged and breathed in. At that moment the four-month-old fetus inside her opened its eyes for the first time and reached out and touched the warm wall of her belly.

MAREK ŠINDELKA was born in 1984 in the Bohemian town of Polička. He attended Charles University in Prague, majoring in Cultural Studies, and the film academy, FAMU, where he studied screenwriting. He debuted as a writer with the poetry collection *Strychnine and Other Poems* (*Strychnin a jiné básně*, 2005), which was awarded the Jiří Orten Prize. He has published four volumes of prose since: the novels *Aberrant* (*Chyba*, 2008) and *Material Fatigue* (*Únava materiálu*, 2016), the short story collections *Stay with Us* (*Zůstaňte s námi*, 2011), both of which received the Magnesia Litera Prose Book of the Year Award, and *The Map of Anna* (*Mapa Anny*, 2014). A regular contributor on literature to a number of periodicals, Šindelka lives in Prague.

NATHAN FIELDS (1977) was born in Oceanside, California, and studied Literature at St. Francis College in Brooklyn, Writing at California State University San Marcos, and Anglophone Studies at Metropolitan University in Prague. Since 2002, he has translated widely from Czech, both fiction and non-fiction, short stories and novels, entire books as well as contributions to anthologies, periodicals, art catalogues, and exhibitions, such as for the Museum of Metropolitan Art in New York and Expo 2010 in Shanghai, China. His recent translations include the novel *Nahr Al-Bared – Cold River* by Jana Kotaishová (2014) and *Glare* by Jan Čumlivksi (2014). He lives with his family in Prague.

A native of Zlín, Moravia, PETR NIKL is a Czech visual artist, puppeteer, occasional musician, and performer. A recipient of the prestigious Chalupecký Prize for young artists in 1995, he has had numerous exhibitions in his home country and abroad. His work often incorporates theater, live performance, and play, and in this vein he developed the concept for The Garden of Fantasy and Music that was part of the Czech pavilion at Expo 2005 in Aichi, Japan, and the collaborative Orbis Pictus and Labyrinth of Light project, which traveled the world.

ABERRANT

Marek Šindelka

Translated by Nathan Fields from the Czech *Chyba*,
originally published in 2008 by Pistorius & Olšanská

Design by Silk Mountain
Set in Janson Pro with Futura titles
Artwork by Petr Nikl
Cover by Dan Mayer

This is a first edition published in 2017 by
TWISTED SPOON PRESS
P.O. Box 21 – Preslova 12
150 00 Prague 5, Czech Republic
info@twistedspoon.com
www.twistedspoon.com

Printed and bound in the Czech Republic by PB Tisk

Distributed to the trade by

SCB DISTRIBUTORS
www.scbdistributors.com

CENTRAL BOOKS
www.centralbooks.com

10 9 8 7 6 5 4 3 2 1

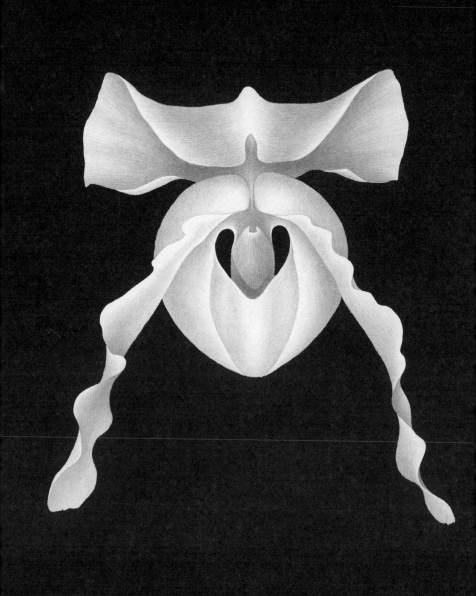